FEBRUARY 2025 - ISSUE 221

FICTION

NON-FICTION

Neil Clarke: Publisher/Editor-in-Chief
Sean Wallace: Editor
Kate Baker: Non-Fiction Editor/Podcast Director

Clarkesworld Magazine (ISSN: 1937-7843) • Issue 221 • February 2025

Bodyhoppers
ROCÍO VEGA, TRANSLATED BY SUE BURKE

I

They wake up in a body that isn't theirs, repeating a series of words. *Dragonfly, laser, twenty-three eighty and two domino.* They open their eyes. The pastel pink paint on the walls hurts to look at. The body is sound, the retinas intact; what's new is the mind.

They breathe.

Breathe for the first time in weeks. *Dragonfly, laser, twenty-three eighty and two domino.* They need to write it down before they forget. They sit up. Deep within their skull another consciousness is vibrating, clawing at the brain, trying to hold on. A primal reflex, obviously. Everyone does it when they're expelled, as if redirection to another organic or mechanical body within two hours wasn't assured. The struggle doesn't last long. In seconds, the other consciousness dissolves.

They pull out the neural jack and stroke their thumb over the metallic circle around it. It feels so smooth they smile. They know it's easy to get lost in sensations, but they can't wait too long to write down the combination. Hopping is usually traumatic. They have to find a way or they'll forget it.

They stand up, stagger, and swipe their hands over the flat surfaces in the room, accidentally knocking over a figurine of a clown and a digital portfolio that bounces on the rug but doesn't break. They almost tip over the bedside lamp. They open drawers and trip over sneakers. A desk. They grab a pen from a stand and open a drawer to search for a notebook, a pad, a tablet, anything. *Dragonfly, laser, twenty-three eighty and two domino.* A block of bright-colored Post-its. The top one is phosphorescent orange. Dragonfly, laser, twenty-three eighty and two domino. Ready.

Ready.

1

They breathe again. Next to the door is a mirror. They step closer to find out more about the body they've invaded. It's been a long time since they pirated one like this: in its early twenties and, except for the neural connector behind the right ear, no evident modifications. The body is fairly lean with strong lungs and a good pulse. Judging by the quality of the furnishings and the quantity of gadgetry all over, they wouldn't expect otherwise. Nice bodies aren't cheap. They like what the ex-occupant has done with it: hair dyed green and violet with matching nail polish. They smile. When they had their own body, they liked to paint their nails, too. They touch their face, their lips, taste the lipstick.

They stop and look at themself with reproach. They shouldn't waste time distracting themself with touch and taste. They should remember who they are and their purpose. It's the only thing that matters.

"River," they say aloud and place a hand on the reflected chest. "You are River. Look for Beam. Follow the instructions."

They can't waste more time. The intrusion has probably been detected already, and if not, it will be soon. They open drawers and closets stuffed full to overflowing and find a backpack big enough to hold everything they think they'll need: a wool cap, a scarf, underwear, a pair of pants, and three shirts. They haven't felt cold for a while, but they haven't forgotten that organic bodies can die from it.

Next to the bed is a smartphone and the node to the virtual Net, which they disconnect, turn off, and disable methodically. They remember seeing a tablet in a drawer while they were searching. It's old, but it still might be worth something. They pack the photo case and a portable video console that they salvage from a shelf and, on the vanity, they find a box full of jewelry that seems authentic. The person they expelled from the body has a considerable collection of makeup and nail polish. They don't know how to use it and don't believe they can sell it, but on an impulse they stuff a couple of bottles in their backpack because the colors look pretty. They also take the manicure set. They'll need that later.

One last time, they turn on their heels and scan the room. They aren't wearing shoes, so they put on the sneakers they tripped over when they got up. They put on a coat, slip the backpack onto their shoulder, and leave the room, not knowing what they'll find on the other side of the door.

They're on the second floor, and the hallway is wide and bright. White wood doors. Brown wood floor. The air smells of varnish and lavender air freshener, the perfume of their body, and clean clothes. They want to kneel and touch the wood grain, the fine joints between the boards, and savor the bitterness of the wax with their tongue.

There's no time for that. Trouble is coming fast.

They grab the banister and start down the stairs afraid that the cerebellum they still don't quite control might betray them. The door to the street is ahead.

"Janet, are you going? I thought you'd stay until this afternoon . . . " a voice from below says.

They stop, and as they do, they realize they make a mistake. There's a body in the doorway between what seems to be the living room and the entryway. It has long red hair and the color of the skin and eyes don't match theirs, but it's wearing a housecoat and the voice seems familiar. When they look at each other, there's no turning back.

"You are not my sister," the body murmurs, their face choking with rage and fear. "Hey, Iris!"

The housekeeper shouts and comes running.

"A pirate! There's a pirate in Janet's body!" the red-haired body shouts and throws itself at River as they are leaping toward the door. River doesn't want to do them any harm but can't let them notify the people at Progress. Pirating bodies is punished by erasing the offending consciousness. The red-haired body grabs their backpack and tugs on it frenetically. "Iris! Shut the . . . !"

River shoves back hard. The body hits the wall and whimpers. Flesh feels pain. River snatches up the backpack and turns the doorknob. Iris hasn't digitally locked the door. They run out without looking back, through a yard surrounded by a white fence, and the lawn stains their shoes green. They wish they could stop and feel the fresh grass.

They run. Their breath catches in their throat. It hurts. Their veins burn, full of adrenaline. It's wonderful to have glands that secrete hormones. They smile and keep running.

This is life.

The body can run for an hour and a half, but they pause before leaving the residential neighborhood to rip out the Micro-ID. They hide behind a trash bin, pull off the backpack, and take out the manicure set. After they wash the space between their thumb and forefinger with acetone, they sink the little curved scissor blades into the soft skin where they felt the Micro-ID. Blood flows into the wrinkles on their wrist and down their sleeve. They dig until they find the metallic lump and pry it out. They're tearing up. The pain is as intense as ever, but each time River gets better and faster. They see the chip rise up and pull it out with their fingernails. It leaves a big hole that they cover with a cotton ball to stop the bleeding. They put everything into the backpack, pull it onto their shoulders again, and start running.

They are no longer nobody.
Now I am me.

II

The city screams at me with neon lights and honking horns. It's all so strident, the air so full of stink and toxins, that when I get downtown in the afternoon, I'm ready to pass out. My veins aren't filled with adrenaline anymore, and my muscles throb with lactic acid. The hole in my hand burns so much that when I let my mind wander, the pain eats at me. I'm dying to sit and rest, but now is not the time. The orange Post-it keeps repeating: Dragonfly, laser, twenty-three eighty and two domino. I remember what to do. My survival depends on it. The first step was to take out the Micro-ID so they couldn't find this body, and the second will be to change my network chip to locate Beam. For that, I need to find Dragonfly.

It won't be easy, but I expected that. I grit my teeth and start walking.

I slip into the ant-like swarm of people and avoid bumping into anyone so they don't look at me twice. For now, my only disguise is the cap and scarf, so I cover my face up to the bridge of my nose in case I pass a surveillance camera without noticing. The facial recognition software isn't that good, and there are always a lot of people with face masks and filters, so I won't stand out if I don't do anything odd.

Electronic billboards greet me as I go by. I don't have a Micro-ID, so there's an uncomfortable silence between "hello" and the rest of their pitch, which makes them sound even more fake when they assault me with red and yellow alerts and promise offers I can't refuse. A new phone, clothes, an enchanting week at a vacation complex, the latest single by a group I don't know. They offer a complete selection of bodies to choose from. The Asian look is now fashionable, they say: the ad reverts to the latest single, and five Korean singers prance around the Progress logo. *Minds matter*, the three-note corporate jingle, an orange knife-thrust, and then an ad for washing machines.

I know I've left the gentrified neighborhood when the ads stop offering me bodies. They offer me money in exchange for mine.

"Hello, do you want to live forever?" That's how almost all of them start. They were playing this game even before I joined the program. "What if we assured you it's easier than you think?"

Someone once told me it seemed incredible that after all this time, the ads for the Progress leasing program have hardly changed. After all

4

the evictions, the Winter program, the furious videos uploaded into the Net . . . even after the first lairs were broken into and the bodies were pirated. The ads haven't changed because they work, because people still need the service. A family member gets ill and you can't afford the medical care, or you want to send one of your kids to the university, or your car breaks down and you need it to get to work, or you want to open a business . . . They promise you that as long as you pay for your monthly installment you won't have a problem: if your body breaks down, they'll give you another one. And if you don't want to live in this reality, there's a place for you in one of the Virtual Nurseries *(As Real as Reality Itself)* where you can interact on the Net as if you were still using a neural jack.

Of course you expect to return to your body, or a body, although you signed a fifty-page contract filled with abusive clauses because you've convinced yourself they won't apply to you.

And then, it happens.

There's always a problem because the system is designed to create them. When you talk to people like yourself, you learn that your story isn't new: at some point, it all goes south. You're now not eligible for a slot in the Virtual Nursery, and you can't return to your body because it's occupied by someone with more money than you have. Now you have no home.

Of course, the Corporation can't eliminate a consciousness. The law says so. But the law lets the Corporation put us into forced hibernation. They turn off your consciousness and your ability to think or feel, so being immortal is the same as ceasing to exist.

Beam and I were there. We waited almost three years to wake up, until the Nobodies pirated our lair and liberated our consciousnesses. Many were lost, but some of us managed to flee. We are bodyhoppers. Criminals, fugitives, terrorists. We're whatever they want to call us. But we're alive.

And, fortunately, we aren't entirely alone.

Dragonfly's workshop is in a grimy building. The front windows have been walled up from inside. I know this is the place because three marks are scratched into the metal doorframe. They're like the symbols hoboes used on doorways, only for people like me. I knock with my good hand and wait. Eyes peer out from a slit. I show my injured hand and wait. Locks and bolts are pulled back, and the door opens. The body that greets me has a burned cheek that a dense beard can't quite hide. They wear worn scrubs under a gray medical coat. They point a gun at me.

"I'm River," I say, and I take off my backpack. "I'm looking for Dragonfly. I need a laser treatment."

They frown and lower the gun.

"I was told you'd come. You're going to have to wait."

I nod, although they're not paying attention anymore. They let me in and glance at the alley before shutting the door with six locks. None of that will matter if a corporate patrol comes with drones and explosives, but I suppose it makes the clients feel better. Inside, the air reeks of iodine and disinfectant. All the light bulbs except for one hang loose from their ceiling fixtures, and the floor and furniture are clean. I'm not alone in the waiting room: an adolescent body sitting on a badly upholstered chair gives me a glance. Their hand is bleeding like mine. Are they a pirate too, or just someone who wants to escape from their own identity? They keep watching as I wait on the other side of the room. I'd like to talk, show some interest in them . . . but I know that neither of us trusts the other because we can't let anyone know who we are.

"River," someone calls from an examination room.

Dragonfly is using the same body as the last time I saw them, but they've implanted better eyepieces. I can tell by the lumps under both eyes. I smile automatically when I enter the room, and they reach for a handshake.

"I got the message," they say, "although I thought it would take you longer to get here."

"The body was in a suburb. I came on foot." I shrug off the backpack and show him my loot. "This is everything I could take before they caught me."

I kept a few rings and a gold chain in an inside coat pocket, just in case.

Dragonfly tilts their head, unsatisfied.

"It's harder every time," they murmur. "Progress monitors a lot of network chip movement."

"You can't leave me like this." I swallow. Blood has drained from my cheeks and the hair on the back of my neck is standing up. "I need you. Beam is waiting for me."

Dragonfly nods. "I know, I know. We can let it go this time, but you're going to have to make it last." They look at me hard, and I wonder if they're recording this conversation with their eye implants or if they're only monitoring my vital signs to make sure I mean what I say. "No promises of help for the next body. They're almost on to us, understand?"

I wonder whether the conversation would have been the same if I had brought more valuables.

At nightfall they open my skull and replace pieces of neural hardware. I don't have a mirror to watch, but I know what they're doing because

I've seen this kind of operation already. It's more like fixing a computer than surgery, but it's still dangerous. A mistake with the instruments or static electricity could fry my brain, and while I'm sure Dragonfly knows what they're doing, a lot of others out there don't. It's difficult work, but lucrative: there's always someone who needs an illegal replacement part or a new Micro-ID. The next time (because there will be a next time) I hope to run into one of the good technicians.

I hope Beam found one, too.

When the operation is over, I'm put in a recovery room to rest. Other people are there; I can see their feet but not their faces. Before I close my eyes I look at the combination I kept in my pants pocket. The rendezvous is still on.

For hours, I drowse restlessly. Every time someone enters or leaves the recovery room, I open my eyes to make sure they're not coming for me. My legs uncramp. Next to the cot is a bottle of water to drink. My stomach rumbles, but I can keep ignoring it for a while. Hunger is agreeably disagreeable, just like sleepiness or the need to pee. After spending so long unable to feel what others take for granted, pain is an existential-level pleasure.

III

"River, you're good," Dragonfly says to wake me up.

I sit up, light-headed and dry-mouthed. I grab the bottle and gulp it down; my nose and throat sting, probably because their pink mucous membranes have never had to cope with such dense air pollution. When I find Beam, we'll need to get some filter masks. I plan to follow Dragonfly's advice exactly.

"I need a node," I murmur, my voice thick with phlegm. "Do you have one here?"

They shake their head. "Use a street node. There's one a couple of blocks from here that usually works."

I give them a dirty look. I told them I don't have anything more to sell, although that's a lie. Without money, how can I use a street node? Dragonfly shrugs because they understand what saying no means: without a node, I can't find Beam.

"I didn't notice this," they say, pointing at the mess I made taking out the Micro-ID. "Come on, I'll close it up."

They take me to an exam room, numb my hand, and close the wound with a stapler that sounds like gunfire. My heart races. A drop of blood

7

flows lazily down the base of my thumb. Before it falls, I lick it off. I've been a full day without food, and it tastes delicious. "Do you have something to eat?" I ask while I savor the metallic salt of my own blood.

"Wait." Dragonfly turns pale. They drop the stapler onto a table and grab a pistol from a drawer. They don't say anything or look at me. They don't need to. Maybe I misinterpreted the noise earlier. When I hear it again, I know what it means.

"River, get out!" Dragonfly shouts and secures the door with a digital lock, then an analog lock. "That way!"

They point at a door that connects this exam room with the next one. I grab my backpack from a chair and swing it onto my shoulder as I run into the next room, which is empty except for hissing refrigerators full of drugs and organic replacement parts. My instinct is to fill my backpack with more valuables, but the shouting out in the hallway makes me dash through another door that takes me to the waiting room. The same body is there as before, as stunned and scared as me. No one has to tell us something's wrong: we have to get out of here.

I hold my head and rush to the back. The other body is right behind me. Someone broke down the front door, maybe a corporate patrol, the police, or thieves hoping for a safe full of money. It doesn't matter. From the doorway come shouts, threats, and bangs, but I don't look as I run down a hallway. No one told me there's an exit, but I know it exists because it's not the first time I've had to escape from a place like this. My legs and head hurt. We look left and right, barge into a bathroom, and run past an operating room where someone was left with a half-connected cybernetic leg.

The emergency exit has a sideways latch, the kind that pushes open. The other body shoves it and runs. A billy club smacks their face. They fall to their knees, bleeding, and look at me. A gloved hand grabs the back of their head and slams it against the ground. I don't stop. Someone shouts at me. More gunshots. The walls of the alley echo as bullets graze them. I scream.

Run!

You always have to keep running.

IV

It's easy to hide in a city if you're nobody.

At dawn, rain drums on your head and the asphalt. Light becomes less artificial and more intense, and the blue and white glare of display panels is replaced by a dirty yellow tinged with red that hurts your eyes so much you squint, blindly navigating the back streets in search of a pawnshop.

This will never change, River. You know it. You're going to spend the rest of your life, a life that will end only when they catch you as a pirate hopping from body to body, trying to keep feeling like you exist in the real world. You and Beam could have accepted the offer that the Nobodies offered when they woke you up from hibernation. A lot of people do, and there's nothing wrong with that. You both could have continued to exist in another virtual Nursery, a pirated one, exploring immortality risk-free, free from desperate scrambles, always just one step ahead of Progress and the police in order to live a little longer. Free from pain, free from exhaustion.

But you both said no. You said you'd rather try your luck in the real world because it was the only life worthwhile, because you knew that virtual refuges come to an end. You'd rather exist with uncertainty, difficulty, and danger. You'd rather be able to touch and kiss each other with real hands and lips for as long as possible. And when the time comes, perhaps die.

Perhaps die.

It's funny that you'd both consider dying acceptable although you began all this to escape virtual death. Yet for you, it all makes perfect sense.

The sign on the store is dark, but the door is open. You keep your head down as you pass the security camera, wipe your shoes on the wet doormat, and try to decide if the clerk will ask too many questions or call the police. Probably a list of stolen goods has been posted, and that's how they'll catch you. Every movement is a gamble, but you can't stop. Beam is waiting for you.

You cough as you come up to the counter protected by double bulletproof glass. Behind it is a bent old body in a thick coat. The store has no heat.

"I want to sell this," you say, trying to be forgettable, insignificant. With your good hand, you hold out the jewelry you kept. "Will you take it?"

The body drags their wheelchair over and leans forward, gesturing for you to put the jewelry in a little metal box for evaluation, and reaches for a scanner. They give it a quick check, barely touching it, and the equipment beeps and chirps. Their lips purse in a way you can't interpret, and your heart speeds up. Maybe they've recognized one of the pieces. Maybe it's all over.

They turn the scanner to show the price on the panel. It's not bad. You agree and wait. They turn their chair to charge a card with the agreed-on price. After more clattering and chirps, they take the card and put it in the box, still warm, as they remove the jewelry and give you a receipt. You glance at it to confirm the amount loaded on the card before leaving as fast as you can.

You deliberately walk for a half-hour, just in case, before you dare to hunt for a street node. On the way, you stop briefly at a soup cart and ask for a large cup, drinking it so fast and eagerly that people move away as you pass. You have to force yourself to drink slowly because it wouldn't be the first time you vomited after the first good meal, but even so you've finished it before you find a node booth. You toss the cup into a wastebasket, wipe your grease-covered hands on your coat, and enter. You lock the door, sit down, pay with the money card, and insert the jack behind your ear.

A magnetic hum shakes your teeth to the roots, and the counter starts running. You close your eyes and can still see it: that's what happens when you connect to the Net. You're here, in the booth, in the city, and at the same time, you're everywhere. The microprocessor in your brain gives you this kind of omnipresence, browsing servers and accessing information through a simple bright interface that luckily is already up to date. You read the social network trends and the latest news, and learn that since the last time you checked, there have been three terrorist attacks and a subway accident, the kidnapped daughter of the president of France was rescued, and the war between China, India, and Pakistan probably won't end this year. Complete arm and leg implants are fashionable ever since Jaz-Q showed off his new arms in the MTV award ceremony, so a lot more operations are expected next year. Another chunk of Antarctic ice collapsed with a corresponding rise in sea level.

All this in one second as people come and go on the other side of the booth's frosted glass.

Somehow your brain doesn't explode from the massive information upload. Somehow, your mind overlooks it and only notices the snippets that matter. They carry you to an obscure corner hidden behind a password. You read the Post-it and repeat it in your mind, twenty-three eighty and two domino, and a door opens and you find Beam's message. It's brief, only some numbers and letters that you easily decipher and interpret. Now you know where to go. You delete the message and hope you can trust the chip inserted by Dragonfly so no one will trace what you read.

You disconnect and end the session. The booth doesn't return your money, but that's fine. Hope bubbles in your belly. Hope and a greasy broth full of additives.

On the bus, you let yourself sleep soundly enough to dream.

Consciousnesses don't dream on the Net. Not in the lairs or the Nurseries. They don't need to. The mind resists resting if it's stimulated, and stimulation never ends on the Net. There's always some news or a fresh idea to share and evaluate, or to swallow and digest without even tasting.

Bodies are slaves to their pineal gland. In the rattling bus, with your coat draped over you, your eyes close. Despite the uncomfortable seat, the moisture condensing on the window, and the muttering of other passengers, the purr of the motor lulls you into a deep, sweet sleep, nothing like the confused drowsing in Dragonfly's workshop.

Ever since you left your own body, dreaming is an experience. You lose the control provided by the virtual world, and at times you forget that what you see and feel isn't real, which is what makes it so different. You return to places you forgot and combine them with others you still remember into impossible locations. You reencounter people from the past, people you called family when you still shared blood types and genes, as if that means something in a world where identities can be dumped into servers. You laugh, cry, go mad with fear, and wake up in the same place you were a moment ago, as if you'd disconnected from a session that turned too intense.

There's still a ways to go. You shift in your seat, but you don't feel like sleeping again. You're so close to Beam you can feel it, so anxious you clench your jaw until it hurts.

It's stupid, right? It is. But . . . what if this time . . . ?

What if this time you can't find each other?

The thought nestles into the base of your skull on top of the processor. You fight it by recalling earlier times, weeks spent happily together until they tracked the two of you down. To survive, you had to throw yourselves into the Net like fish dying on the bank of a river. That thought brings back the anxiety of virtual drifting, months spent apart when you were nothing more than bits trying to console each other, unable to caress. You fear finding no more bodies to hop into. The next one might be the last. Death, but dying badly, alone.

Don't think about this. You're almost there. Hang on.

Hang on.

You take your backpack and get off at your stop, a half-abandoned seaside town, its land being swallowed up by water. You buy a sandwich from the only store still open so late and head toward the last bit of the seaside promenade that hasn't been devoured by the sea. A precarious walkway, lapped by high waves, leads to a graffiti-covered stone pavilion crowning the headland. A wave breaks near the rocks and splashes against the rusty railings, and cold spray lashes your face. You lick your lips and savor the taste of the ocean. As you approach, you spot a colorful glass mosaic decorating the pavilion beneath the graffiti. You smile. If Beam chose this site, then they know it. It bears their mark, their appreciation for the little things, the nice things that work so hard not to disappear.

You wait. The sky is overcast, and the clouds and air pollution produce strange colors as the sun sets. The tide goes out. You lean on the railing and notice that low tide has revealed a tiny beach. The sand shines in the lamps along the promenade.

You have to feel it under your feet.

You climb down from the headland and take off your shoes and socks. The sand is icy cold, and sinking your bare feet into it makes you wince and almost yelp. You notice stones and shells dragged in by the tide among bits of glass and plastic bottles stained by seawater and sunshine. You sit on the broken foundation of a handrail and wait.

You wait.

The roar of a motorcycle makes you look up. It comes from the other side of the promenade, from the road not yet covered by water. You stand up and stuff your hands under your armpits as if the cold sand had suddenly become too much to bear. The motorcycle stops a few meters from you. An unknown body gets off it, tall and fat, with close-cropped hair and thick lips. They smile at you. You walk toward them, not caring as the asphalt scratches the soles of your feet. They open their arms, and you let yourself be wrapped in them, bury your nose in this new unknown scent that imprints itself into your memory to replace the one that had been there until now.

You take their cheeks in your hands, rub their jaw with your thumbs, and feel the texture of their hair and the softness of their ears. You clasp their body in an embrace. You absorb their warmth, their physique, the curve of their hips, and the pressure of their embrace. You kiss their lips and savor the taste of their mouth, and when you breathe together, every doubt you had disappears.

You're back home.

Originally published in Spanish in *Cuadernos de Medusa I*,
published by Amor de Madre, 2018.

ABOUT THE AUTHOR

Rocío Vega writes science fiction and fantasy. She won the Best Short Story and Best Anthology Ignotus Award for *Compañía Amable* and has also published the Horizonte Rojo novelettes and several stories in anthologies and magazines. She is a big fan of video games and TTRPGs, and sometimes plays and rants about them online. Rocío lives in Spain with her spouse and two cats.

Sue Burke is the author of the science fiction novels *Semiosis, Interference, Usurpation, Immunity Index,* and *Dual Memory.* In addition, she's published short stories, poetry, journalism, and essays. She's also a translator, working from Spanish into English, for such writers as Angélica Gorodischer, Maria Antónia Marti Escayol, Sofia Rhei, Josué Ramos, Juan Manuel Santiago, Eduardo Vaquerizo, and Cristina Jurado. She's currently in Chicago but had the pleasure of living in Spain from 2000 to 2016.

King of the Castle

FIONA MOORE

"We wouldn't mind Feargal living in the Big House," Naomi said, refreshing Morag's cup of tea, "if he would only keep to himself. But he killed one of Rhiannon's sheep, and he pulled a knife on young Christine."

"Not a bad thing to stop that girl playing round the Big House, though," Morag spoke more lightly than she felt, trying to play down her own worries. Naomi ran the village post office and read a lot of books, and so was the person people went to when they needed a representative or spokesperson. Morag, five years her senior, was the person people went to when they needed something fixed, in both the real and the more metaphorical sense. And she wasn't sure if this could be easily resolved. "It's dangerous there, even without Feargal."

She couldn't resist a glance at Seamus, who was sitting in front of the hearth of Morag's farmhouse in power-saving mode, its six digitigrade legs folded under its blocky body. She'd found Seamus up on the spoil heap, the old mound of slate, rubbish and old tech from back when people had thrown things away without thinking about it. But Seamus had once been a defense robot at the Big House, and nobody could deny it could handle itself in a fight, for all its delicate, tottery appearance.

"I thought you and the other salvagers had stripped the place of tech."

"Not all of it, and there's more dangers in there than just tech. Falling walls, rotten floorboards. Foxes and wolves."

"Anyway, we're worried he'll escalate. That he'll hurt or kill somebody. Or, on the other side of it, get himself hurt or killed. Christine's Dad's muttering about retribution—I talked him out of it for now, but next time it could be a nomad child, or one of their sacred animals, and you know the nomads don't always abide by our rules."

"I'm worried too," Morag said. "Given what Feargal tried at midwinter." She didn't have to elaborate. Four months previously, Feargal had been the leader of a band of thugs who'd come west from Shrewsbury, trying to set up a feudal state in the hillsides: farmers paying him and his men for protection, or paying another sort of price if they didn't. They'd managed to put a stop to it, in the end, and the village had gone back to its usual vaguely anarchic state.

But things like that left scars. Morag didn't like having a possibly-homicidal man in the Big House, and she especially didn't like the way this was poisoning people's minds, making them think about vengeance and murder. How did you deal with someone like that in a place with no laws, no justice system?

"Why's he still here, anyway?" Naomi complained, passing the scones.

"Good question," Morag said. "I'd expected him to vanish off somewhere after his followers deserted him. I mean, most of *them* joined the nomads, or took up work as farmhands, or went back East licking their wounds. I thought he'd do the same."

"Maybe he can't cope with failure. Or being beaten by a lot of nomads."

"And farmers," Morag pointed out. "And some of those archivists from Portmeirion turned out to be pretty handy with those big sticks they use to smooth paper." Something occurred to her. "It could be he's still here because this is . . . home, for him," she said slowly. "He came over here from Ireland to work for Call Me Steve—sorry, I mean, for the billionaire in the Big House." Call Me Steve had been what the staff all called the billionaire, behind his back, but they generally hadn't used the nickname around outsiders, so she wasn't sure Naomi knew about it. "Twenty, thirty years ago. Wherever he's lived and whatever he's done since . . . it could be this place has left a mark."

"I think I remember him from then."

"What, Feargal? Really?"

"Yes. Ginger kid, wasn't he? Some of the mercenaries from the Big House used to come over to the practice field on rugby night, kick the ball around with the locals." Naomi was the coach of the local rugby eleven, and had been a pretty good winger back when she'd been young.

"I never knew."

Morag had been one of the abovementioned mercenaries, technically. The billionaire who'd bought the Big House, or Gwydion Manor as it was officially known, had hired local young people to supplement the largely Irish and Eastern European security force he'd brought in as part of his plan to use the place as a bolt-hole when civilization collapsed. Morag and Feargal had worked together, sometimes, patrolling the house or fixing the security robots, but they hadn't been friends enough to talk about each other's hobbies. He'd regarded her as creepy, and she'd regarded him as a bully, and that was the end of it.

And, as the billionaire himself had been fond of saying, no plan survives contact with the enemy. After a couple of years, the food began to run out and the billionaire began to talk about sending his mercenaries out to exact tribute from the local people. Morag had quietly removed the restraint programming from the security robots. Stood back and watched the billionaire, his wife, and his captains all die in a hail of bullets. Not her, though. Not the billionaire's kids, because she'd got them to safety. And not Feargal, he wasn't important enough.

Morag had been too busy after the disaster, looking after the billionaire's kids and coming up with a narrative for the villagers about what had happened, to care about what happened to Feargal. He'd disappeared off into the countryside, somewhere. But now a lot was falling into place. The village, the Big House, were home; the billionaire his mentor. So of course he'd developed a fixation. Had to become a feudal lord, like the billionaire wanted to. And especially, had to become a feudal lord *here*, to show everyone who'd laughed at him.

And now he was defeated, he still couldn't walk away.

Morag filed the train of thought. "You'd think playing rugby would help, I mean, isn't learning how to cope with failure part of becoming an athlete?"

"Yes, well," Naomi said. "If you wouldn't mind having a word with him, it would be helpful."

"But why me? You know he's a violent man." He'd been a bully as a kid, an obsessive as an adult, and, if he was killing animals and threatening children, he was getting worse. "Why not Owen, or Ross, or one of the other big fellows?"

Naomi shrugged. "You've got Seamus."

"That I do."

"And he might be more reasonable with someone he doesn't see as a threat."

"Don't know that he doesn't see me as a threat. I'll do what I can, but no guarantees that I can do any better than anyone else."

"I know you're in there, Feargal." Morag decided to be direct. "So do the rest of the villagers, and we're none of us too happy about it."

Silence, behind the thick door. It was made out of some material supposed to be blast-resistant, though there'd never been occasion to test that.

Morag reflected that, if Feargal was going to hole up somewhere, he'd picked the best spot in town to do it. The Big House had been built as a manor in the eighteenth century, and, even if the floors were falling in, the walls were still standing. From the looks of it, the west wing was uninhabitable, gutted by fire and with buddleia growing from the windows. But part of the east wing, on the ground floor at least, was solid, and had easy access to the cellars.

"All right then," she said loudly. "Coming in another way." She turned, walked along the side of the house towards what had once been the kitchen. Sure enough, she found the trap door to the cellar partway along. With a bit of help from Seamus, she was able to pry it open and climb carefully down the stairs.

"Feargal?" she called again once she reached solid ground. The cellar wasn't well lit, but enough daylight came in through the high slit windows that she felt safe enough, particularly with Seamus at her back.

A scuffling sound, like rats, further down the cellar. Then a harsh, feeble voice called out, "you'd better be armed, witch."

"I'm not," Morag said. Seamus was, arguably, and, back in the courtyard, Naomi was waiting with a stick in one hand and a whistle in the other, ready to call for help and come in swinging if she heard sounds of trouble, because Morag wasn't stupid enough to come without backup, killer robot or no killer robot.

The room was full of storage shelves, most of them bare, and the only reason the shelves themselves hadn't been removed was because they were made of aluminum, and no one in the village needed that enough to take the trouble. Down at the other end, she could see that he'd set up some kind of defensible encampment, building barricades out of trestle tables and storage boxes. Beyond that, she could see into the next room, which looked to be more residential; the shelves had been cleared out of that one, and she could make out a camp bed, storage boxes, lanterns. Some bloody lumps that she assumed were what was left of Rhiannon's sheep.

And other things.

Stacks of tech. It couldn't have all been from the house; he must have been foraging out on the hillsides and spoil heap. Monitors, keyboards, pads, phones. Drone parts. A couple of cute dog-shaped robots Morag thought might have belonged to the billionaire's kids. All static, unmoving.

"And I'm sure you aren't, either," Morag went on. "I've been over this place for years, and none of the weaponry's usable. Gunpowder's got a limited shelf-life, and Call Me Steve believed in technology over durability. All those flashy laser-sights and automated target locks don't last long in the damp. They're not even useful to salvage for microchips."

Before her conscious mind could register the sound of movement or the shift in the air, she ducked. The gun butt missed her by inches. Seconds later, the body of Feargal also missed her by inches as it slammed into the floor, pininoned spread-eagled by four of Seamus' limbs, while it braced itself on the other two.

"I thought it was a good idea to teach Seamus a few non-violent defensive routines," Morag said, very calmly. "I've been a farmer long enough to know that even sheep can turn into fighting machines when they've got their heads trapped in a fence." She waited a few minutes, then crouched down by him. He looked stunned; he'd probably hit his head on the stone floor.

Good, Morag thought.

"I haven't come to force you out," she said, slowly and clearly. "That's not the way it works around here. But how it does work is, if you do want to stay here, and you don't want to do anything useful, you've got to at least be harmless. So no scaring the children or killing animals that aren't yours, understand?"

She ignored the text of Feargal's reply, as she had the general idea.

"Let him up, Seamus," she said, deliberately turning her back to show she wasn't afraid. "We're going."

Once she was outside the cellar door she sagged against the kitchen wall, getting damp blackish slime all over her coat but not really caring. She hadn't been sure how well Seamus' defense routines would work against an actual hostile human, as opposed to her nieces and nephews trying pretend attacks on her and each other. And seeing Feargal again brought back too many bad associations, too many feelings of anger, and of injustice. It wasn't fair that he was still up there, demanding everyone's attention and not letting the village move on. It wasn't *fair*.

Fair's for kids, Morag reminded herself. Grown-ups just have to accept that things are what they are, and work with them. If he feels like this place is home, then it's home. She looked over at where Seamus was standing, the energy in its limbs giving it the sense of something poised on tiptoes. Reminded herself that Naomi was outside, that beyond her in the valley were her neighbors, her friends, her family. A village of maybe twenty houses, plus a pub and a post office, but it was alive.

She was okay. She had her people, her community. Feargal had nothing.

• • •

"I have to give him credit," Morag said, perusing the hacked-together array of technology topping the Big House's walls, "he hasn't done too badly."

"He's electrified the main gate," Naomi said. "And got the cameras working."

"Not the cameras," Morag said. "The proximity sensors. That's what got the milk-cow the other day. It triggered a deadfall." The animal had broken its leg and had to be put down; chalk up another victim of Feargal's crime spree. "Give him credit, he listened when I said the guns wouldn't work. Problem is, he's been rigging traps that don't involve them."

"Either way, what do we do about it?"

"We wait," Morag said. "I give it five to ten minutes."

They waited in silence.

A few minutes later, the cherry-red lasers stopped sweeping the area in front of the gate, and the gate itself audibly powered down. Seamus came trotting back through the gate, almost nonchalantly.

"That's the thing with those robots," Morag said, raising her voice a little in case Feargal was nearby. "The Big House's security systems automatically recognize them as friendly. I didn't even have to teach Seamus a new routine: turns out 'disable security systems' is in there already."

"How much more of this do we have to put up with?" Naomi asked as they walked back down the hill.

"I don't know," Morag said. "We'll have to work something out, though, before he tries again. He's gone from threatening people to actually trying to hurt them, and that's not good."

"What I wonder is, why he doesn't go back to Ireland if he doesn't like it here," Dai the brewer said. He, Morag, and Morag's brother Zeb were sitting at an ancient picnic table out back of the brewery, field testing Dai's latest experiment in dark ale and watching Seamus play football with six of Zeb and Dai's orphans. Morag had a cat on her lap and a dog of indeterminate parentage sleeping on her feet, and a cockatoo that had somehow found its way into Zeb and Dai's household was pacing up and down the table pushing a walnut about.

"Send 'em back where they came from?" Zeb raised an eyebrow at his husband.

"You know that's not what I mean." Dai smiled, conciliating. "But the people who come here and stay, stay because they want to or because they had no other choice. He could always go to Caernarvon or Porthmadog and hire a boat to take him to Ireland."

"The fishing fleet don't go out that far."

"Glyn does, if you pay him."

Morag half-listened, thinking. Zeb wasn't her brother by blood; he was one of the billionaire's children. Both of whom had grown up here, become so much a part of the community that nobody thought of them as anything else. Zeb's sibling had even joined the local nomad tribe, the Children of Flame. And, for all he'd done wrong, the option to stay was open to Feargal. Most people in the village had done something unspeakable when things started breaking down in the cities; often several somethings.

Home, she thought. For some people it's a thing to rebel against, to fight. Maybe that was why he was up there like a cargo-cult Call Me Steve. Maybe he had the same feelings about the place he came from; maybe he couldn't go back till, in his mind, he'd proved himself.

"Rabbie's doing well," she said as one of the broader teenagers managed to stop a kick from Seamus.

Zeb beamed with pride. "Rabbie just made the rugby eleven," he said.

"Really? That's fantastic," Morag said. "I remember you were so worried about him."

"After that incident with Tom the Pole and the watering can, I thought we'd have to send him away. But Tom wasn't angry. Next time he came by on his rounds, he brought a rugby ball and taught Rabbie some drills."

"And that worked?"

"He's channeling all that negative psychic energy into beating the other kids. And most of the adults, too."

"Shame we can't do that with Feargal," Morag said. Then she frowned. "Maybe we *can*. Let me have a word with Naomi."

Morag generally didn't take much of an interest in sport, and only turned out to watch when she knew it would make family or friends happy if she did. Nonetheless, she showed up to watch the rugby eleven practice on the field behind the spoil heap, with Seamus and an ancient folding chair.

Sure enough, by the time the team were warmed up and doing kicking drills, a scruffy figure emerged from the quarry road and came to join them. A couple of the players pulled back, muttering, but Naomi said something to them, and they let him join in.

At the end of the practice, Feargal disappeared just as quickly, and Morag went over to talk to Naomi.

"Well," Naomi said. "I didn't think he would, but you were right."

"Is he any good?"

"No." Naomi winced. "He was okay back in the day, but now? Hasn't got the reflexes, hasn't got the knees."

"I'm sorry," Morag said. She'd left a bottle of Dai's dark ale by the door of the squat at the Big House, with a note affixed. The note contained two pieces of information: one, the times of the local rugby practices, and two, details of how to get in touch with Glyn (a note at the hotel bar in Porthmadog, or else at the Black Buoy Inn near Caernarvon's wharf, usually did the trick) and arrange travel to Ireland.

Now, though, she felt disappointed.

"So he's no good, then?"

"Didn't say that." And Naomi suddenly smiled. "He's got knowledge."

"How do you mean?"

"I couldn't really see it at the time, but now, well. My guess is, he probably played rugby at a decent level when he was younger, maybe when he was a kid, a teenager. Then dropped out later on. It happened a lot, back then, with professional sports. People didn't make the cut, or they got injured, and got advised to find a career elsewhere."

"That makes sense," Morag said. "He never really talked about his past, but none of them did. I could see him starting out in sports, getting rejected, joining the army instead."

Naomi's smile turned sarcastic. "Not being able to handle the discipline, quitting and taking a job at the Big House."

"History doesn't repeat itself, but it does rhyme." Morag couldn't resist a glance at Seamus. Non-violent routines, she thought. A killer robot can become a guardian. Or, thinking of how it had been playing with her nieces and nephews the other day, a footballer. "How is it Feargal knows things you don't? You've been playing rugby for years."

"As an amateur. In a local team. But Feargal, he knows how they used to train back before things fell apart. When there was an international rugby league, top level education. Sports science. He can't play, but let me tell you—he could teach."

"That might be what it takes," Morag said. "To bring him in, if he won't move on. If all of this behavior is down to some anxious need to be in charge—then give him a title, call him the coach, get him teaching the team what he knows."

"And maybe we'll actually make the finals this year."

"Wouldn't *that* be grand."

Weeks went by with no further incidents from the Big House. The spring rainstorms came and went. The rugby team practiced. The villagers and Feargal began to get used to each other. A few of the rugby players took to giving him food and clothes. Making sure he was okay. Morag began to relax. The wound in the village was closing, beginning to scar.

Then, one day on the border between late spring and early summer, Morag was helping Tom the Pole—who was tall and skinny, and Polish, and carried a staff like a nomad, so no one was sure how he got the nickname—load boxes of preserves and cheeses from her farm onto his wagon to sell to the grocer in Porthmadog. Abruptly, Seamus leaped up from where it was exposing its dorsal solar cells to the cloudy sky. It stood in the doorway, braced, the melted lump on its front side that might have once held a camera, or a claw, or a gun, tilting wildly about. Morag never quite knew how it could sense trouble so accurately, but she'd seen it react to things happening too far away for her to hear or see, and it had never been wrong about them.

Seamus raced out the gate, and by the time Morag, closely followed by Tom (who had taken a moment to grab the staff from inside his wagon), had made it up the hill to the sports field, it had Feargal pinioned in its nonviolent restraining posture.

Rabbie was breathing heavily, leaning on Naomi for support, and nursing a swelling face.

"You're off the team," Naomi said to Feargal, with menace.

From the ground, Feargal sneered. "You said, you need what I know."

"I don't need it that much," Naomi said. "Be nice to have an edge in the spring championship, but not if you're going to go feral. Pack up," she said to the rest of the players. "Practice is over, and we'll use the field by the school next time." She gave Morag a significant look.

Rabbie hesitated. "Is it okay, just leaving him on his own like this? What if he does something?"

"If he does," Naomi said, "then you have my permission to hit back." But she turned to Feargal. "Leave us alone, you hear? You just exhausted your welcome in these parts. I don't care where you go or where you live, but I don't want to see you again."

Seamus maintained his position until the team had gone, at which point it cautiously released Feargal and trotted over to Morag and Tom the Pole.

Feargal just lay there.

Tom the Pole dropped out of his defensive stance, shouldered his pole and started to walk back to his wagon.

"You're just going to leave me here with him?" Morag demanded. "Why do people think he's *my* problem?"

"You don't have to stay here with him." Tom the Pole stopped, turned back to her. "You've done what you can, as have we all. He's only your problem if you want to make him your problem."

"True," Morag said, realizing it. Then, "I feel responsible, though. Go on, I'll meet you back at the farm."

She'd been the one who tried to give him a second chance, to bring him in the community. That was a mistake, and now it was on her to try and fix it.

As Tom left, Morag walked over to Feargal. Squatted down. Then sat, because it was easier on the knees.

"What happened to you?" she asked. "This isn't acting like a soldier. Or a sportsman. This is just lashing out."

"I want to go home," Feargal said.

"Here can be home," Morag said, "if you want it to be."

Feargal said nothing.

"If you mean you want to go back to Ireland, I told you how."

Feargal didn't answer that one. Then he said, "is this all there is? Of all that was?" Before Morag could parse the sentence, he was going on. "Nothing's left of it. The tech's decaying, the data's gone. Those footballers . . . back in the day we had drugs, and doctors, and algorithmic training routines, and practice robots. These kids got nothing like that. Just their bodies and their minds."

"Isn't that all any of us have?"

"People in the future will think we couldn't write. Or draw. Nobody can read digital files anymore." That wasn't strictly true—there were a few devices still around—but Morag wasn't going to correct him on a technicality. "In twenty years there'll be no trace. There's more left from the *Victorians* than from us."

Morag shrugged. "Is that a bad thing?"

Feargal smiled. "Aw, but it was beautiful, wasn't it?"

"I lived out here all my life, except the first few years," Morag said. Her family had come south from Scotland when the flooding got too bad. "And I don't feel I missed much."

"You fix tech," Feargal sneered. "Aren't you being a hypocrite?"

"I fix tech, yes," Morag said. "But none of it works like it was originally intended. I wire solar cells into drones so they don't need batteries. I turn grass-cutters into mowing machines for the farmers. I teach Seamus nonviolent restraint techniques, and the kids teach it football moves. And yes. In forty, fifty years' time it'll all be gone. Maybe even Seamus will be gone." She had troubling dreams, sometimes, of Seamus in the archive at Portmeirion, motionless on a shelf in the room where they kept the taxidermy. Or staggering around the hills, alone, like when she'd found it, slowly wearing out and falling to pieces. "But there'll be new things to replace them."

She looked at the spoil heap, at Seamus standing at a convenient distance from her and Feargal. Its claws were deployed, a warning of what it could do if it wanted. But also a reminder that it wouldn't use them, unless she or someone else Seamus wanted to protect was threatened.

"Knowledge," she said. "Knowledge lasts. So long as people remember how to make a thing, or do a thing, it's out there. Even if you're not, anymore."

Feargal scoffed.

"Which is to say that, if you're worried about nothing you've done ever lasting, then remember, you taught the rugby team. And they'll teach younger players. And younger ones."

"What happens when we're all nomads?"

"Nomads still play ball." She saw the Children of Flame sometimes, whirling around the practice field with an old ball or an inflated animal bladder. Ritual or game, she wasn't sure: with the Children it could be either or both. "You've seen kids playing that game, King of the Castle? One kid gets on top of the heap and the others have to knock them off, and then the one who succeeds becomes king? Well, the world's not actually like that. You're standing on the heap, daring someone to knock you off. But there's no one. No one else wants to play the game anymore. You need to think about that."

Seamus shifted its claws in and out, warning.

Feargal sneered. "Better get back to your protector."

Morag didn't bother dignifying that with a reply. She left him on the field.

"We could try using force?" Tom the Pole suggested as Morag rejoined him. "Get up a mob, chase him out of the Big House?"

"I don't think he'll be any more trouble today," Morag said. "Let him alone. I think he'll move on when the message finally sinks in."

But somewhere in the back of her mind was a worry, about what he might do before that happened.

Back when Morag was small, rugby teams would play against each other at pre-arranged times, over a number of weeks and months, culminating in a championship. Which, given the erratic state of communications in a world where you were dependent on drones, nomads, and Tom the Pole for the delivery of messages, wasn't really something they could do any more. So, by general agreement, the local rugby teams all gathered at the playing-field at Caernarvon at midsummer, since everyone could agree when that was, and camped out there for several days, playing each other until finally, one team was the victor.

Most of the village would go along for all or part of the session, some to support the team and some just for the excitement of the trip. Morag would go herself sometimes, if she could find someone to mind the farm for the duration, to meet friends from more distant towns.

This year, especially, she thought it might be worth the effort. Time to renew acquaintances, strengthen ties. Feargal hadn't been seen since he'd been kicked off the team, and the events of midwinter were starting to fade into memory, but all the same, Morag had a feeling.

So she called in a favor with Owen, joined Zeb, Dai, Rabbie, and some of the other orphans, in their brewers' cart, and went up to town.

"I really don't understand it." Morag's sort-of-apprentice, Cliff, said to her as they ate goat-meat kebabs on a hill by the stadium. Cliff was a nomad who made the rounds of the local villages, where he sold plans for useful machines, and sold his own services building and repairing those machines. "This man tried to take over your town? Threatened you? Tried to kidnap you, personally, at least once? Pulled a knife on a kid? And you tried to make him your *sports coach*? Wouldn't it be better to just drop him down a sinkhole?"

"Believe me, I wanted to," Morag said. "But that's not how we do things round here. And we've all done things that would make our neighbors want to drop us down a sinkhole."

"All the same. He seems like a risky person to put that kind of trust in."

"That's why I'm here," Morag said. "Oh, to see you, and Maya and Saoirse from Portmeirion, and to cheer on Rabbie, and all that. But I'm worried, too. Worried he might do something."

"You said he wasn't up at the Big House anymore?"

Morag nodded. "No one's seen him there for weeks. Ross had a look in the cellar and said he couldn't find any evidence the man was still around. But I don't think he's got what he wanted. And I'm worried he might come here and cause trouble."

"How could we find him in a crowd like this?"

"Good question."

"Hm. Do you think Seamus might . . . "

"Good thought." Remembering Seamus' uncanny senses, Morag turned to the robot and, feeling a little silly, crouched down by its front end as if she were speaking to a dog or a small child. "Seamus, can you find Feargal?"

"Does it know his name?" Cliff asked.

"It's not stupid. It can put together words and context."

The little robot stood for a moment, raising and lowering its scarred front end. Then it trotted off purposefully.

Towards the part of the stadium that had once been the spectator stands.

With a sinking feeling, Morag stood up to follow.

"Stay here," she told Cliff, who was doing likewise. Then, "No, actually. Come to the door of the stands, and wait there. He might be spooked if there's more than one of us, but, if things go wrong, backup is a good idea."

"Put the gun down and come away from there," Morag ordered.

The little robot had led her through a maze of back corridors until finally stopping in front of a small maintenance room in the eaves. Morag had spent the journey thinking of what someone like Feargal might do with a high perch in the stands, so she was not unprepared for what she saw once she opened the door.

She could see Seamus sidling, waiting for the command. Which made her feel less afraid, though she didn't doubt Feargal could get off at least one round before Seamus could get him down. But she held off. Knocking him down might stop him beating up Rabbie or hitting Morag, but it clearly didn't do much to solve the wider problem.

Feargal at least looked away from the small, arrow-slit window and the old rifle. He must have found some historic ordinance in the Big House, Morag thought, hidden away so the salvagers had missed it. The kind that the Victorians made. To last. And got his hands on some cartridges for it somehow. Maybe trading with one of the farmers who made their own, or stealing . . .

Later, she'd have to go up to the Big House and make sure there wasn't anything the local kids could use to hurt themselves. But for now, there were more urgent matters.

"Make me," Feargal said.

"You know I can," Morag said. "And I'm not doing it. Think. Is this really what you want people to remember you for? A massacre on Rugby Weekend?"

Feargal smiled nastily. "But they'll remember me."

"For heaven's sake, man, before you do that, *look at the field*." Morag, without thinking—without letting herself think—stepped forward. "Look what they're doing."

Feargal did lower the gun, though keeping it ready in his hands. Looked out at the field. Frowned. Said nothing for a while, as the multicolored dots down below whirled around the field and the chorus of happy singing from the lower part of the stands broke into a mix of cheers and groans.

"They're doing what I taught them."

"More than that," Morag said. "Look at the shirts." Uniforms were a thing of an earlier era when cloth was cheaper and easier to get, so teams usually distinguished themselves with colored shirts that they could also wear to work in.

"What am I missing?"

"*That's not the village team*," Morag said. "That's Ffestiniog."

Another pause. "I don't believe it."

"The village team colors are blue and white. You've seen it. Ffestiniog are green and gold."

"How?"

"You want to be remembered? You will be. The techniques you taught the village team are being learned and copied by the other teams. They'll spread to the whole island. Maybe out to the continent, eventually."

"You think?"

Feargal turned, slumped against the wall. The tension gone out of him.

He put the gun cautiously down on the floor. Rested his arms on his knees, like he was thinking.

Once Morag was reasonably sure he wasn't going to do anything stupid, she reached out and, matter-of-factly, took the gun. Opened it, removed the cartridges.

"I can't go back to Ireland," Feargal said.

"Yes, you can. You're ready."

"I don't have any money."

Morag resisted the impulse to scoff at the obvious excuse. "Glyn will take work, or trade." She put the gun back down, pocketing the ammunition. There was the risk that he might still have some on him, but somehow she doubted it. "Give him that gun. He won't have any use for it himself, but he can sell it to a farmer or to the archive."

She left him in the room, though, once she was out of earshot, she asked Seamus to do a quick sweep of the corridor for anything containing black powder or shot. Just in case.

"How'd we do, in the end?" Morag asked Naomi, as they wandered in search of a ride back towards the village, and prepared themselves for the long walk if they couldn't find one. After the confrontation with Feargal, she'd walked a long way from the stadium, took an even more roundabout way back, and wound up drinking with Cliff and Glyn in the wharfside district, finding her way back to the campsite after the others had gone to bed.

"We made the semifinals," Naomi said. Morag had guessed they'd done pretty well given that Naomi didn't appear to have slept, but not how well. "We got beaten by Criccieth, but then, the big town teams have the advantage of more leisure time and better organization." After a bit, she said, "Do you know what's happened with Feargal? I know he left the Big House, but nothing more."

"I checked at the Black Buoy," Morag said, her face neutral. She'd sworn Cliff to secrecy about the previous day's events. "Word is, he made a deal with Glyn, and they'll have been off across the sea at last sailing." Which had been at about five that morning.

Naomi sighed with relief. "At least that's one problem sorted. Did he catch the rugby final?"

"Apparently," Morag said, still keeping a straight face.

"I wonder why he stayed? He could have gone off to Ireland any time."

Morag shrugged. "He probably had to move on in his mind before he could move on with the rest of him. Maybe the rugby final was part of that."

"It's a shame it didn't work out. He could have had a good career as a coach—"

"Don't think it," Morag said. "He knew things from before, yes. But he had a temper, and always had to be in charge. You can't do that and be okay around here."

"You're right," Naomi said. "I shouldn't make the past better than it was."

"And the team have learned what they need to, and they'll put that to use. The best part of him stays here, the rest goes on." She didn't know if going back to Ireland would help him, but it was a good thing that, if he couldn't make the village his home, he was now out there trying to find some place he could.

"Oh look," Naomi said, pointing, "there's Dai and Zeb and the kids."

"We'd better hurry," Morag said, "if we want to get a lift back with them."

ABOUT THE AUTHOR

Fiona Moore is a BSFA Award winning writer and academic whose work has appeared in *Clarkesworld, Asimov, Interzone,* and six consecutive editions of *The Best of British SF.* Her most recent fiction is the short story collection *Human Resources* (NewCon Press) and her most recent non-fiction is the book *Management Lessons from Game of Thrones.* Her publications include one novel; five cult TV guidebooks; three stage plays and four audio plays. She lives in Southwest London with a tortoiseshell cat which is bent on world domination and a sealpoint cat which is not too bothered.

We Begin Where Infinity Ends
SOMTO IHEZUE

Atop a ladder was Naeto, reaching for the lights. The lights flickered as his touch neared. Down below, Gozi held the ladder, rooting it to the ground. A small breeze came, and the ladder tilted, and the ladder swayed, but Naeto did not waver. Gozi was down there—Naeto knew the ladder would steady.

Over the school break, around midnight, the two boys had secretly been recalibrating all the streetlights in their town sector. There were fifty streetlamps on the asphalt road winding down the outskirts of the Asaba sector. Naeto and Gozi had changed fifteen since they began.

"The both of you are always tinkering."

Gozi spun around, letting go of the ladder. Naeto's legs gave way as the ladder buckled from under him. Before he could come crashing down, Naeto leaped for the streetlight's pole, the adhesive suction of his gloves activating. His hands now clasped safely around the pole; he slid down. The ladder had fallen but not touched the ground.

A girl had caught the ladder.

The light from the streetlamp illuminated her face: Bushy eyebrows, wooly brown hair squashed under a baseball cap, and freckles scattered across her face—the brown of old sawdust. Her shirt was an alarming white. Her cargo dungarees were torn at the knees. One of its straps rested on her shoulder. The other fell free. And the girl was tall. Taller than Naeto, but not taller than Gozi. Nobody was taller than Gozi.

"What are you doing here?" Naeto pushed past Gozi, throwing him a semi-angry glare. Gozi would answer for letting go of the ladder and almost killing him, but first, the girl.

"What am I doing here?" The girl squared up, her face inches from his. "What are YOU doing here?"

While Naeto agitatedly adjusted his glasses, she just looked on, slightly amused.

"We—We—" Gozi began to stutter.

"None of your business." Naeto did not let him finish. He grabbed the ladder she was still holding. The girl did not let go. Naeto tugged at it, and she held on tighter, a smile building on her face. Then, she let go, giggling as Naeto stumbled back, nearly knocked to the ground. Naeto cursed under his breath before placing the ladder back against the light pole.

"Hi." Gozi lumbered next to the girl, scratching the back of his neck.

The girl narrowed her eyes at him. "Hi."

"Gozi!" Naeto called in a hushed scream. A startled Gozi rushed forward with confused and asking eyes. Cedar-brown eyes. Naeto sighed, holding the bridge of his nose. "Hold. The. Ladder." He punctuated every word. "This time, try not to let go."

Gozi steadied the ladder once again as Naeto climbed back up.

"You still haven't explained what you're doing?" The girl waved from behind them.

"We don't have to explain ourselves, least of all to you." Naeto dislodged the streetlight's casing. This was a newer model, and screws were not employed in its fastening. The ones with screws took longer to dislodge.

"Maybe you'd like to explain to the security patrol."

Naeto stopped. The girl could not physically thwart their operation, but the security patrol could—and it would not be the first time.

"We are re-calibrating the lights," Naeto gave in, letting the light's casing hang loose as he began poking through the electrical circuit of the fluorescent tubes. The lights flickered with every touch.

"Re-calibrating?" The girl crossed her hands over her chest. "Why?"

Naeto did not respond. He reached into the chest pocket of his overalls and pulled out a diode filter. He connected this to the circuit bridge, and the light's sheen went from radiantly harsh to something softer.

"That's why." Naeto gestured to the soft light.

River. That was the girl's name. Since he was eight, Naeto had won the Young Engineers Builder's Prize three years in a row. He lost the prize after River and her parents moved into their sector a year ago. Naeto was distraught for weeks. River didn't know the things he knew about mechanical equilibrium, satellite motion, and thermodynamics. But, somehow, she had won the prize by building an unfinished canoe. Naeto always made sure to emphasize the unfinished part. And, unlike him, she never seemed to be trying. She would skip class to go skip pebbles across the lake, paint unartistic murals on the town council's walls, or work on her unfinished canoe. *What twelve-year-old went around building canoes?*

River blinked at the soft light, a question gathering in her eyes.

"It's for the fireflies." Gozi excitedly answered the still-gathering question. "It's saving them."

River slightly cocked her head at him. "There are no fireflies . . . " She looked up from Gozi to Naeto, who quickly shook his head at her. " . . . not here anyways."

"Because the harsh lights keep hurting them," Gozi muttered.

"Wait." Naeto clambered down the ladder. "You should not have been able to see us." He tugged at the translucent fiber overalls both he and Gozi were wearing. Under illuminance, he had designed them to confer a measure of translucency. He had made them after the security patrol caught them the last time.

"You're tinkering right in front of my bedroom window," River pointed to her house across the road. "I can't sleep with the lights going on and off every second."

"Maybe, next time, don't live on the outskirts of a sector, away from civilization," Naeto suggested.

"Maybe, next time, don't design ugly malfunctioning overalls," River suggested back.

"They are adequately functional." Naeto's voice cracked and pitched a hint higher. "And we are engineers, our outfits are designed for practicality, not beauty." Naeto had spent sleepless weeks on those overalls and, up until that moment, had believed they were the most beautiful pieces of clothing ever.

"Engineers without safety gears? Not even a climbing rope. I am in awe of your combined brilliance."

"Well—well, I'm not an engineer," Gozi said, offering an unsolicited clarification.

"What are you then, big boy?" River sent a smile his way.

And Gozi smiled back. "Well, Naeto says I'm more of an assistant."

"And who made Naeto chief supreme engineer?" River scoffed.

"Don't you have things to do? Like a canoe to finish?" Naeto started to take down the ladder. Gozi rushed over to help. Naeto brushed him away.

"Have you been spying on me and my boat?"

"Boat? It's barely a raft."

"Naeto." Gozi tried to stop him.

Stopping was antithetical to Naeto's character. "And who goes around building a canoe? Nobody uses canoes anymore."

"Didn't you get in trouble for messing with these lights before?" It was a standoff, and she was winning. "I heard your parents got a fine from town council for property damage."

"It's town council that's damaging everything!" It was Gozi.

Naeto had never heard or seen him like that. And from the shocked, remorseful expression on Gozi's face, the big boy hadn't either.

"I'm—I'm sorry—"

"Who is there!" It was the security patrol. Their flashlights split through the unlit parts of the road.

"Let's go!" River grabbed Gozi, who grabbed Naeto.

"My ladder—" Naeto made to pick it up.

"Leave it!" River yanked Gozi forward, and the big boy yanked Naeto away from the ladder.

The three teenagers ran, past River's house, ducking under palm fronds, sneaking through back-ways, and scampering away from barking life and mech-dogs. They ran past the lake, the loud chirping of the water bugs drowning out the slapping of their feet against tar. They ran past council hall, River's mural of a whale painted across its walls. They did not stop until they got to Naeto's house. The house was white and shaped like a box.

"Your house looks like a fancy sugar cube," a winded River announced as she studied the building.

"It's minimalist." Naeto realized he and Gozi were still holding hands. He let go. "And you didn't have to follow us all the way, your house was across the street."

"I needed the exercise." River faked a stretch. When she was done, she just stood there staring at the boys.

Naeto hoped she would turn and leave at some point. She did not.

"I've never been in your house before." River hopped onto the metal stairs that led to the front entrance.

Naeto hushed her. His father was a light sleeper. River hushed him back.

"Do you want to see Naeto's workstation?" Gozi shied in, low and eager.

"Yes!"

"No!" Before Naeto could protest further, Gozi had taken River from the door to the side of the building. Naeto grudgingly followed. There was a scan box lodged into the wall. The big boy grabbed Naeto's unwilling hand and placed it against the scanner. The scan box identified Naeto's prints, and a ladder whirred down from the window to the ground.

"You really are a fan of ladders," River chuckled to herself.

Up the ladder and inside Naeto's room, the girl looked around, trying to hide her awe, and failing.

"Look at all this . . . tinkering stuff."

Naeto's room was hexagonal and large, like three regular bedrooms merged into one. And there were things everywhere—but in a tidy, orderly manner. Workbenches lined with digital worksheets, shelves stacked with jars, huge manuals, and several "high-tech" appliances. A holographic board was sectioned against a wall. Mini wind vane rotors, solar panels, and engine motors were stacked on the floor. River leaned against one of Naeto's adaptable workbenches. She touched something, and the bench morphed from a smooth drafting table to a low magnetic field, attracting and pulling small metallic objects to its center.

River cupped a giggle.

"Please don't touch anything," Naeto sighed from behind her.

She ignored and waltzed over to a smart tool rack shelved over a wall. The rack held a plethora of unfamiliar materials. River took a jar from a row. Inside was a glowing, weird looking stone.

"Is this radioactive?"

A robotic arm snaked down to her and retrieved the jar.

"GeniT does not appreciate disorganization." Naeto took the jar from the robot and placed it back on the rack.

"Where did you get all this stuff?"

"Naeto's dad is one of the biggest scientists in the country," Gozi squeaked in.

"Don't over-embellish," Naeto said, rearranging the rack.

"I don't know what that means."

Naeto sighed. "It means—"

"Do you want to see something cool?" Gozi turned to River.

River nodded expectantly.

"We don't need to show her everything." Naeto rubbed his forehead.

"Do it," Gozi pleaded, tugging at Naeto. "Please, please, please."

Naeto exhaled, rolling his eyes. "Fine." He looked up at the ceiling. "GeniT, *starlight!*"

Starlight, GeniT beeped back in a mechanically velvet voice.

The room went dark. But only for a moment. Across the ceiling, across the walls, tiny pinpricks of light came, gradually intensifying until a sea of stars burned alive. The constellations followed, in shimmers, tracing stories in the bright dark. A meteor sped across the pocket universe, and River's eyes followed, and the lights found her pupils, illuminating them. And the planets, in subtle hues of red, blue, and brown, came orbiting into view—the rings of Saturn, the stormy swirls of Jupiter, and the burning of Mars. And galaxy folded into galaxy, and planets uncharted came, with black holes rising and coming undone. And there wasn't one sun, there were suns. A hum filled the room. It was still and gentle, like space itself had birthed it. And River reached out, her hands going higher, higher, and River touched infinity.

"Did you do this?" The girl's eyes did not stray from the stars burning across the digital planetarium.

"Naeto did." Gozi looked over to Naeto.

Naeto took off his glasses and started to clean them. They did not need cleaning. "It's just crap I put together and—"

"It doesn't look like crap to me." River, too, was now looking at Naeto.

And at that moment, Naeto thought her eyebrows were not all that bushy.

"Naeto could put one in your bedroom if you liked," Gozi offered.

"No, I can't."

"Why not? You did one for me."

Naeto did not answer. His eyes shifted from Gozi to River, and back to Gozi. The three of them stayed like that for a minute, a triangle with quiet edges.

"Is this the re-calibration thingy you were talking about?" River broke the quiet, walking over to one of the workbenches. On the table were circuit components of a streetlight broken up into sections.

"We're filtering the lights." Naeto joined her. "We added a diode component to yield softer lights—starkly different to the radiating intensity of our streetlights."

"The streetlights are too bright," Gozi explained in simpler terms. "Too harsh. It makes the fireflies' mating glow invisible. They also can't hide from predators because the lights give them away. And what happens when they can't hide or make baby fireflies?"

"They go away," River answered calmly, a calmness Naeto didn't think she possessed. "But fireflies are already . . . extinct. I read it in the National Geographic—"

"No, no, not extinct. Just very endangered." Gozi brimmed with nervous excitement, eager to share this new information. He rushed off to the holographic board and tried pulling up a page. "There have been firefly sightings not far from here, in the Ogbunike caves . . . " Gozi's hands were sweaty, and the moisture interfered with the board's functionality.

"Let me do it." Naeto nudged him aside.

"If fireflies still live in these places, maybe they still live . . . or can live here. They just need a little help." Gozi let out a breathless giggle.

"So, unlike the harsher lights, yours doesn't confuse the fireflies?" River turned to Naeto. "They can differentiate between it and their own lights?"

"It's still a prototype and needs more research, but yes, we think it could possibly, probably, help save Gozi's fireflies." Unlike Gozi, Naeto tried being more practical with his assessments.

"It's your fireflies too." The big boy gently shouldered Naeto, not gently enough, for it sent him staggering a little.

"It was your incessant idea to save the fireflies, like my schedule wasn't busy enough already," Naeto said, regaining his balance and adjusting his glasses. "I'm only doing this for theoretical research purposes."

"That doesn't make them not your fireflies."

"Let's agree to disagree."

River was watching them, amusement in the corner of her eyes. Again, Naeto removed and wiped his glasses. They did not need cleaning.

And morning interrupted, dawn stealing through the blinds.

"That's my cue." River skipped to the window.

"Your cue was hours ago." Naeto folded his tired arms.

"Same time tomorrow?"

"Yes." It was Gozi.

"No!" Naeto hushed him. "This is not jet club."

"Tomorrow it is." The girl laughed, climbing out the window. She slid down the ladder, faster than they both usually did, and she ran off, sunlight trailing after her.

And it went on. Day after day, River would sneak in through Naeto's bedroom window, and she and Gozi would aid him in fine-tuning his invention. They often just watched, giggling and scheming between themselves, and annoying Naeto. It took Naeto a minute to adjust to this new addition. Gozi, on the other hand, was thrilled to have someone else to talk fireflies with.

"Did you know fireflies are beetles, not flies, and are related to ladybugs and rhinoceros beetles?"

"Did you know firefly eggs also glow?"

"Did you know fireflies use their lights to communicate with each other?"

And at midnight, they would all sneak out to add the filter diode to the streetlights. With the three of them, the operation now progressed faster. River also insisted they used safety climbing gear, and she vehemently refused to be called Naeto's assistant. She did agree to wear the ugly overalls.

One night, they gave her a farlight. Another one of Naeto's inventions. It was how Naeto and Gozi communicated—mostly for the fun of it. When night gathered, one of them would shine their farlight into the sky, and wherever the other farlight was, it would come aglow. Two farlights in the night sky meant they would be re-calibrating the streetlights at midnight.

"Just like fireflies." River carefully took the farlight in her hands.

"Just like fireflies," Gozi repeated, the smile on River's face finding his.

River's glee faded. "I live far away. Your lights won't find my light." She handed the farlight to Naeto and backed away. "I also don't think I'll be here for long."

River's parents were research archeologists. They moved around a lot and had lived in many sectors.

"My family is from Rwanda," Gozi bridged the space between them. "I was born there. My moms say we would go back someday. But that day is not today." He squatted a little to look her in the eyes, just like his moms did when they wanted to reassure him.

"And there's a reason they're called farlights." Naeto folded the farlight back into River's hands. "They might not get to Rwanda or wherever your folks move to next, but here in this sector, wherever you are, it'll find you."

And what was once two farlights in the night sky became three. And what was once fourteen re-calibrated lights became thirty.

"We should give the new lights a name!" River beeped up.

"I agree!" Gozi beeped up too.

Naeto rolled his eyes as he scribbled new schematics on the holographic board. Of late, Gozi had eagerly been going along with all of River's ridiculous antics.

"We should call it The River Naetozi Tinker Light!" River sprung to her feet, hands on her waist, victorious.

Naeto exhaustingly rubbed the bridge of his nose.

"It's our names merged into one!"

"Very original." Naeto stepped away from the board. "But why does your name come first and written in full while ours gets meshed up? Eh?"

"Because I came up with the idea." River leaned on the table across from him. "The lights would still be nameless without me."

"The River Naetozi Tinker Light is a long, ridiculous name."

"I—I like it." Gozi chirped in.

"Of course you do," Naeto scoffed.

"Maybe if you say it over and over, it will grow on you." River danced in Naeto's direction. "Say it. Say it," she began to chant.

"No!" Naeto scampered away from her.

River threw back her head, laughing a bellied contagious laugh, and soon, Gozi joined in. Eventually, so did Naeto.

One night, Naeto fell from the ladder and landed on his arm. It was just him and Gozi. River's farlight had not shone in the sky.

Gozi ran to him. "Let me see." He gently took Naeto's hand.

"It's nothing." Naeto clutched his arm, stifling a painful groan. The gloves' adhesive function had not activated in time.

"We shouldn't have left the safety gear."

Naeto had left the ropes on purpose. "It takes too much time to set up. Time we do not have."

"Now see how we're spending all that precious time." Rarely was Gozi sarcastic. Naeto didn't think he was even capable of it. Despite his hurting arm, this amused him.

"This is not funny," Gozi's voice grew firm. "This is bad."

A purplish bruise was starting to spread across Naeto's arm. Under the streetlight, it was radiant like an overripe avocado.

"I'm sure River will be happy."

"I think she'll be upset," Gozi countered.

A wordless minute passed between them as the big boy inspected the injury.

"We should get you to the clinic."

"Right, and explain how I got injured and why we are out this late?"

"We cannot leave you like this. What if it's some . . . internal injury? What if it gets worse?"

Naeto could tell Gozi was not going to back off.

"Fine. Fine. We'll go to the clinic," he reassured him. "But let's go tomorrow, after I come up with an elaborate lie."

"Naeto—"

"It doesn't hurt as bad as it looks, I promise."

"Are you sure?"

"Ugh, I swear it by the River Naetozi Tinker Light."

River could get Gozi to partake in all her ridiculous antics, but so could Naeto. Gozi was his friend first. He knew how to get him to budge. And as much as Gozi tried to hide his delight from hearing Naeto use the name, the mile-wide smile playing across his lips betrayed him.

"What?" Gozi was trying his best to stay serious.

"What?"

"You're looking at me weird."

"You were looking at me weird first."

"No, I wasn't."

The two boys were quietly laughing now.

"Oya, stand up." Gozi picked Naeto off the ground. "Let's go home.

Unfortunately, the injury was as bad as it looked. Naeto had sustained a non-displaced fracture. And Gozi had been right, River was upset. She paced the length of Naeto's room, lecturing on and on about how they never listened to her. Naeto just stared blankly at her, his arm in a brace and sling. They had told his father he had fallen off Gozi's bike.

With Naeto's condition, the re-calibrating operation fell to River and Gozi. River was a quick study—which she claimed had nothing to do with Naeto's horrible teaching skills. Adding the filter component to the streetlights became her primary responsibility. They would rendezvous at Naeto's house, with clear schematics and directions on replicating the filter's design. At night, Gozi and River would recalibrate the streetlights using the filters. River also started bringing others. Random kids from school. River insisted that the more people knew about saving the fireflies, the better. So, each day, she showed up with a new kid: Ugochi who endlessly mimicked a hawk's call. Makua and her mismatched socks. Jide who had a birthmark shaped like a tree. Rafael and the clattering rainbow beads in his hair. Nnayeleugo whose laughter was the sound of hiccups. Mazi who spoke six languages. Barefoot Zobam who talked to her reflection and dreamt many dreams. And more and more, they came. If Naeto wasn't losing his sanity before, he was now. Gozi and River were the only ones allowed in his house, and like he always reminded them, was solely because he needed assistants. Now, he had feral strangers—his classmates—running around his workstation, touching all his equipment with unsanitary hands. For Gozi, it was just more people to share fun facts with:

"Did you know firefly larvae eat snails and worms?"

"Did you know that large groups of fireflies sometimes blink in unison?"

"Did you know firefly light can be yellow, green, or orange?"

After a while, Gozi and River stopped showing up as often. To Naeto's knowledge, the operation was still in progress—Gozi had mentioned they set up a second base at River's house since she lived closer to the uncalibrated streetlights. And there was Naeto's father, who was limiting Naeto's "playtime" until he fully recovered, making his house inconducive for their operation. And on days when all their farlights dotted the sky, Naeto would wait and wait, but Gozi and River would not come. Even the random kids from school stopped coming.

Naeto began to feel many things—some he couldn't explain. The recalibration was made possible because of him. The designs and schematics were his. One component wired inaccurately could implode everything. Carrying on without him was unwise on their part. So, he went down to the lake. It was where River held her never-ending canoe construction project.

"Will you ever finish building it?" Naeto asked from behind her, squinting, shielding his eyes from the sunlight.

"We'll see." River didn't look back at him. She was sawing a piece of plywood in half. The cut was jagged.

"That is rather rough."

"A thing isn't beautiful because it is perfect."

That was another thing Naeto found exhausting about River. Her random bouts of philosophical dreamy responses. It was not something she did often, which made it more jarring to witness.

Naeto inched nearer, inspecting the canoe. The places where wood met wood were rough-hewn, bark in patches where the sanding was unfinished. The faint scent of wood sap tickled his nostrils and settled on his tongue. It was pine. Across the planks were paint smudges where River had attempted artistry and failed. The hull had uneven boards held by nails undoubtedly scavenged from a landfill.

Naeto had never seen a canoe on the lake. The floating pads and high-rotor ferries had replaced them all. Things were different in the last sector where River lived. For one, they had canoes. Naeto wondered if her canoe would take to water.

When River was done, she walked home. Naeto followed. She was five steps ahead, him five steps behind, the setting sun a painting on the horizon. River would throw questioning glances at him as they walked, and Naeto would look away. He had never been alone with her before. Gozi was always there. *Why didn't he just confront Gozi instead?*

River lived by the lake. So, the walk was a short one. When she ushered him through the front door, Naeto found the house odd. He had never been inside it before. There was one table. One chair. One portrait of something on fire. You could tell whoever lived in it wouldn't be there long. On the table were bits and parts of the filter diode—River's workstation.

"Where did you get these materials?"

"I stole some of yours." River was beside herself with pride. "Mine is not as sleek as your design, and I don't have an ultra-modern workstation, but it gets the job done. We have recalibrated three more streetlights."

Naeto clinked his fingers on the table, examining the components. Her putting all this together with nothing but stolen scraps and a screwdriver, was fairly impressive. Naeto didn't start with scraps. His father was a robotics and electromechanical systems expert and Naeto had considerable access to his gear. He wondered what River would accomplish with the access he had.

"Did you want to talk about something?" River brought his attention back to her.

Naeto straightened up. "You and Gozi should not have replicated the designs without me."

"Oh," River paused. "I thought he mentioned it to you?"

"He—he did."

"And that you were okay with it?"

"I was."

River let her confusion show, then started to tinker with the filter components. "Also, the rains are back, and the storms have gotten worse this year. We haven't had the chance to re-calibrate the lights in a while."

"Doesn't explain why your farlights have been in the sky these past few nights." Naeto brought his hand between the components on the table, halting her tinkering. One of River's brows climbed in response.

"That had nothing to do with the recalibration, we were just having fun."

"Good to know you've both been doing that too."

River paused again.

"I don't think this is about the lights." A smile tugged at the corner of her lips. Her amusement riled Naeto.

"You—you can't just go around taking people's friends!" He said it before realizing how pathetic he sounded.

"Well, I thought I was your friend too. Apparently not."

"That—that's not what I meant—"

"And Gozi is not property. He is not something to take or give." There was a shift in her tone. "And it's not my fault he likes me more than you."

She was baiting him. He had known her long enough to understand that. Still, he fell for it, all sense of reason flying out the window.

"Maybe he wouldn't if you stopped flirting with him every five seconds."

River snickered. "I'll flirt with whomever I want."

"Good for you! Find someone else then."

"Who? You?"

Naeto went quiet as stone. The question had come like a boulder falling into his open palms, and he struggled to find balance.

"Oh." River's eyes widened. "You do want me to flirt with you!"

"I—I don't." Naeto was unraveling.

"Yes, you do." River chuckled. She danced up to him, and Naeto staggered back. "This is interesting because you want me to flirt with you, but you also want Gozi to flirt with you."

It was all too much information and accusations for Naeto to register. He had come to confront River, now he was on trial. "I—I don't know what you're talking—"

"Don't deny it. You're not subtle, with your wandering eyes." River was visibly enjoying seeing him spiral. "I just didn't know you were a greedy little nerd."

"I am not a nerd!"

"You invented a light filter for your boyfriend. You are a nerd."

"He is not my boyfriend!"

"Sure." River comically tiptoed forward. "Though, lucky for you, I like kissing nerds."

Naeto fled. He stumbled over the table, over the chair, and scattered out the door, and he ran, River's witchy laughter echoing after him.

Three nights later, after his confrontation with River, unable to think straight without her accusations and witchy laughter creeping into his mind and taunting him, Naeto went to find Gozi.

Perched outside his friend's window, the picking wind flapping at his overalls, Naeto knocked and knocked against the window. Gozi's home was a small bungalow, so Naeto did not have to worry about falling. When the window flung open, a startled Gozi was on the other side.

"Nae—Naeto—"

Naeto pushed past him, climbing into the room. Just like his, Gozi's room also had a digital planetarium across the ceiling.

"I have been knocking for hours," Naeto exaggerated, adjusting his overalls.

"What—what are you doing here?"

Naeto looked up with an angry squint. "I have not seen or heard from you in forever!"

"We saw each other last week."

"That—that's not the point." Naeto shifted where he stood. "Remember the fireflies we're supposed to save together? What happened to that?"

"Naeto, there's a literal storm coming."

"I can see that." Naeto did not appreciate his patronizing tone. He was seldom on this end of their arguments. "Which is why we must go before it gets here." He grabbed Gozi's hand and pulled him along. The big boy did not budge.

"You can't tamper with electricity under the rain."

"I know. I am the engineer here," Naeto threw up his hands, visibly impatient. "GeniT predicts there won't be any rain for five hours. We can achieve a lot in five hours."

"You still have your brace."

Naeto had hoped his overalls would hide it. He had removed the sling to make sure.

"It's fine, it's practically healed." He pulled at his sleeves. "I also brought the protective gear for the ladder," he smiled, dangling the ropes in Gozi's face. "I promise not to fall again."

"Naeto, you can't climb ladders with an injured arm. You can't climb ladders in a storm."

Gozi was speaking to him like he was a child, which they both were.

"Or maybe there's someone else you'd rather climb ladders with!"

"Naeto, what is going on with you?"

Naeto bit at his fingernails. His palms were slick with sweat. He wiped them on his overalls, only to find them damp almost immediately.

"River said that you—that you like her," he heaved out.

"Of course I like her. She's our friend."

" . . . that you like her more than me."

"Eh?"

"Do you?" Naeto swallowed, his voice a crashing LEGO set. "Do you like her more than me?"

Gozi just stood there.

And Naeto continued. "Because I like you, I like you a lot, I think I always have, and when River said it the other day, I was so confused, and I didn't know how to feel, and then she tried to kiss me, and I panicked, and I ran away, and I couldn't stop thinking about her, and I couldn't stop thinking about you, and I just want to know if you've been thinking about me too," Naeto blurted out, ending his monologue by wiping his eyes and running nose with his sleeve, all in one take. This made it worse because the snort mixed into the tears, and half his face was now smeared in it.

"You . . . you call me your idiot assistant all the time."

"Oh." Naeto straightened up. He had not expected that, not after his profound confession.

"I know you don't mean it." Gozi's fingers twisted and untwisted around each other. "I just did not get 'I like like you' from being called that."

Naeto took off his glasses and wiped them with his sleeves. They did not need cleaning.

"I'm changing the lights for you," Naeto's eyes avoided Gozi's, focusing instead on a point on the floor. "You cared about the fireflies, so I did too."

Gozi just stood there.

"I put up your planetarium so we could see the same stars every night." Naeto did not look up at the ceiling. He was still focused on that point. "And I built the farlights, so we would always find each other."

Gozi just stood there.

"Naeto I—I ehm—I don't know. I don't know." That was all Gozi said.

There was a physical aching in his chest. Naeto did not understand it. He hugged himself, cradling his hurting chest, and looked out the window. "I—I'm going to go."

"Naeto," Gozi softened. "You could stay here . . . you could just stay here . . . with me."

And the two boys stood there. They stood there a while. Then Gozi reached for him, trying to knit the space between them, and Naeto drew away.

"Naeto—"

He did not wait for him to finish. Naeto scaled out of the window in one swoop, and he ran.

And the rains came down—impenetrable curtains of water. Naeto waded through it, soaked to the bone in seconds. The streets were dark and flooded, half the streetlights sizzling with damp electricity. The torrent rushing through the road drainage was the sound of waterfalls, and it rattled the metal drain covers. Naeto took the ladder from its hiding spot and heaved it against the light post. And in that moment, his resolve wavered. He wanted to turn and run, run back home, run back to . . . No. He was going to climb. And Naeto climbed up the ladder, rain pelting down on him, each drop a small stone. He got to the light casing and dislodged it, the fluorescent plates also coming free, revealing the green-plated circuit beneath. Naeto could barely see through all the water. He was wet. Everything was wet. He could not tell where his body ended and where the water began. But Naeto had done this many times. His hands remembered. He took out the filter diode and inserted it into the circuit. In the downpour, the streetlight went from incandescent to welcoming, finding all the corners of his wet face. The lights reminded him of Gozi.

And the lights sparked, the glass casing shattered, and Naeto fell, and the ground rushed up to meet him. He crashed onto a drainage plate, and it gave way, plunging him into the rushing current below.

• • •

As the sky unwillingly morphed, giving way to a more radiant intensity and dispersing the deep grays from the previous stormy night, it met Naeto hauling his body down the long, winding asphalt road. There was sand in his hair. Bruises and cuts delicately partitioned his face. His overalls were in shreds, like something caught in crossfire. And they dripped water onto the asphalt. Naeto shook as he walked. When the sun was completely over the horizon, its lights touched the paleness of Naeto's face; it touched his eyes, and Naeto did not blink away.

His glasses were gone, his tools were gone, and he would never see the rope again. Only Naeto remained. When he had fallen into the drainage the previous night, he had latched onto the walls and held on. He did not let go, not until the rains died and morning called.

In the far distance, Naeto saw the possible outline of a person's silhouette. Without his glasses, he could not be sure. But the silhouette soon went from one, to five, to many. They surrounded him.

"We found him!"

"Ah thank god!"

"Where were you?"

"Why were you out in the storm?"

"Why were you out at night, eh this boy?"

The voices came crowding him, and many hands touched Naeto. It was a search party. They were all in raincoats, so they had been out all night. Naeto's father broke through the crowd, hugging him tightly until Naeto's body disappeared into his. He took Naeto's face in his hands. His father looked like he had been crying all night.

"Where is Gozi?" It was Gozi's mother.

Everyone turned to Naeto for an answer he did not have.

"Gozi?"

"Was he not with you?"

"No—no, he wasn't. It was just—it was just me."

Gozi had gone after him the previous night. And when his moms realized he was gone, they had reached Naeto's father. Neither of the boys were with the man. The last contact was River's parents. When they dragged River out of bed and besieged her with questions, she confessed to everything; what she and the boys had been doing all school break. A search party had formed immediately.

With the search for Gozi still ongoing, Naeto was hospitalized. First, they pumped out all the flood water he had ingested. In addition to his unhealed arm, his leg was now bound in a brace. He had severely sprained his leg in the fall. Naeto would not climb again, not for a while. River came every hour with updates on the search. She came even when there were no updates. She'd just sit there with him. Naeto believed everyone blamed him for what happened—for making Gozi go out in the storm. Had he listened and stayed that night, Gozi would not have followed, and Gozi would be here, he would be safe. And even if everyone didn't blame him, Naeto blamed himself. But River did not.

They found Gozi two days later.

The torrents had washed him into the lake. He was found amongst the water shrubs.

"Will they let us see him?" Naeto labored out of bed when he heard the news.

"Naeto—" River tried to steady him back.

"They have to let us see him." Naeto fell, and River caught him. And Naeto cried.

"Naeto, listen, please." River wasn't one to plead. "My parents said Gozi was hurt quite bad."

"What—what does that mean?"

"I don't know." River shook her head, wiping away the brimming tears. "I don't know." She turned. She could not look him in the eyes for what came next. "They're taking him back to Rwanda."

"For what?"

"They said he needs extensive medical care, the type he can't get here."

"Rwanda is on the other side of the continent."

"It is. But Rwanda is Gozi's home, and the rest of his family is there and—"

"No! His home is here."

"Rwanda's medical sector is the leading—"

"No, no!" Naeto clasped his hands over his ears, like he knew what she was going to say, but did not want to hear it.

But River made sure he did. "Gozi's citizenship gives him free access to their healthcare."

Naeto went quiet for a while, his hands still over his ears, his eyes shut tight.

"When are they leaving?" he finally asked.

"Naeto . . . they already left."

Naeto cried all night. He cried the next night, the night that followed, and the night that followed. His best friend was gone, and he did not get to say goodbye.

Naeto spent the coming quiet weeks indoors. His father didn't say it, but Naeto knew he was grounded for life. Naeto was fine with that. He also would not get far given his injuries. He hardly left his bed, and there was now a huge body-sized dent in the mattress. Naeto deleted all the schematics for the filters. He threw the prototypes, the suction gloves, the overalls, and the diode components in the trash. Their ladder had been lost in the storm, and Naeto didn't look for it.

And last of all, he took down the planetarium. It was of no use. He and Gozi could no longer see the same stars.

Naeto tried to reach Gozi every day. His father also helped, trying to contact Gozi's parents. They did reach them, but Gozi was never disposed to talk, and when he was, he spoke very little. Over time, their interactions thinned out.

When the school year kicked off, the doctors recommended home-schooling until Naeto fully recovered. But Naeto's body wasn't the only broken thing. On one of those quiet, broken nights, he lay in bed staring at the starless ceiling. And it came, a light the shape of a moon. It refracted through his window and danced across his ceiling.

It was a farlight.

Naeto scampered out of bed to the window, flinging them ajar.

She looked exactly like she did that first night. Bushy eyebrows, wooly brown hair squashed under a baseball cap, and freckles scattered across her face. Her shirt was an alarming white. Her cargo dungarees were torn at the knees. One of the straps rested on her shoulder. The other fell free.

"River."

She must have heard his voice sink. "Oh, I'm—I'm sorry."

Naeto apologetically shook his head. He stepped back, making room for her as she climbed the ladder, briefly perching on his windowsill. She reminded him of a sparrow. No one had come in through the window, not in a while.

"You know you can use the front door."

"I know," River chuckled, squeezing through the window. His room had not heard a chuckle, not in a while.

Now inside the room, River hugged him, a little too tightly. And Naeto hugged his friend back.

"Thank you."

"For what?" River let go.

"For being here."

River shoved him. The way Gozi usually did, only a bit more tenderly. She hugged him again.

"So . . . I was thinking . . . we should restart the River Naetozi Tinker Operation," she whispered.

"What?" Naeto pulled away.

"For Gozi." River tried to reach back for him, and Naeto squirmed away. "He was right about the fireflies making a comeback in other places. They could come back here too."

"River, that doesn't matter anymore."

"It mattered to Gozi." Her voice went an octave higher. "And it mattered to me. And you."

"I—I don't think—" Naeto paused. He took off his glasses and cleaned them. They did not need cleaning. "I can't climb again."

River grabbed his shoulders and squeezed them. "You won't have to. Not today."

"Today?"

River inhaled before skipping giddily to the window. Naeto followed her. "I brought friends." She pushed the window open.

And down below were all the kids from school—the ones River had been bringing to his house: Ugochi and his hawk call. Makua and her mismatched socks. Jide and his tree-shaped birthmark. Rafael and the clattering rainbow beads in his hair. Nnayeleugo whose laughter was the sound of hiccups. Mazi who spoke six languages. Barefoot Zobam and all her dreams. They all had on overalls, protective gears, and tool bags.

"Turns out they were listening while touching your stuff with unsanitary hands," she mimicked him, lathering her voice with snobbery.

"I—I don't sound like that."

"You do."

"River, it's hardly midnight. People will see."

"Let them see."

The whole thing terrified Naeto. This debacle with the lights got them here in the first place—minus him not taking well to rejection. What if someone fell? Or got electrocuted? Or worse?

"It will be fine." River squeezed his hand. "I promise."

And Naeto nodded, letting go—of all the uncertainty, fear, and things he could not control.

"I doubt they know how to use those tools." He looked down at the pack of chattering kids scattered on his lawn. Their tool bags and overalls were a few sizes too big.

"Oh, it's mostly for the optics. We grabbed what we could from the school lab." There was a tinge of prideful accomplishment in her voice.

"Of course those hideous overalls came from the school lab."

"They are designed for practicality, not beauty." River nudged his shoulder with hers, and Naeto covered his face with shy embarrassment.

"And you can change the name if you want to," River offered. "It's your lights after all."

"Well, River Naetozi Tinker Lights has unfortunately grown on me," Naeto flashed her a half-smile, one that built into laughter. And there they were, two giggling children in a bedroom that once held stars.

So, Naeto, River, and all the kids from their school went from streetlight to streetlight, recalibrating the lights, filtering their glow from a harsh brightness to something soft, something safe. As expected, parents and the sector's security patrol flooded out, trying to stop them. That would have been possible when it was just Naeto and Gozi. Now, they were many. And what was once thirty-three recalibrated streetlights, became fifty.

"Did you know there were once winter fireflies up in Seattle?" River asked Naeto.

"No. No, I didn't know that."

River went quiet.

"My parents are moving again."

"Oh." That was all Naeto said.

"I heard it's nice in Seattle. They have snow. I have never seen snow before."

"River." Naeto's eyes welled up. It was happening again; he was losing another friend.

River's eyes welled up too. It would be the last time Naeto would see her like that.

"Don't you dare forget me, nerd!" She whacked his chest.

Naeto let out a shaky laugh—it was also a shaky sob. "You are impossible to forget. And you're a nerd too."

River thought about it for a minute and nodded in agreement. "I am."

"And you can thank the flickering lights. You wouldn't have seen us that night if not for them."

"That wasn't the first time I was seeing you."

"Oh, really?"

"You're like the least subtle person alive. I knew every flickering light was the both of you."

"So, you'd been watching us?"

River blinked a nod.

"Why?"

"I liked watching you and Gozi." She tucked a stray braid behind her ear. "I liked watching you."

And under the River Naetozi Tinker Lights, River kissed Naeto. A gentle thing. This time, Naeto did not run away.

• • •

Twelve years later and Naeto was going home. Home had been a memory for a while. He wondered if the sector was the same. If the sun still trailed after running children, if the rains still fell like pebbles, and if the streetlights were still soft. He hoped they were. After what he, River, and the other kids had done, they had garnered quite the attention. Media outlets carried the story of schoolchildren culling light pollution in their home sector to save the fireflies. Government agencies and wildlife conservatory bodies followed, with a keen interest in the ecological benefits of the recalibration process. The offers came next: monetary offers from power corporations, partnership propositions from questionable tech founders, and scholarships from renowned institutions. Before long, Naeto was off to college, the youngest in his class. With a highly funded graduate research grant, he put together a team, further advancing the mechanics of the recalibration system. In time, the River Naetozi Tinker light was utilized worldwide in a conservation effort to decrease light pollution and restore the critically declining population of fireflies. Naeto's groundbreaking innovation was life changing. When he graduated college, the job offers poured in. Despite River's remarks about him being a "horrible" teacher, Naeto loved teaching. So, he took a position at the Namibian University of Science and Technology, the same institution he had graduated from, and he was content.

Now, sitting in the back of a haxi—the new hovering taxis everyone was obsessed with—Naeto was going home. Because Gozi was there.

They had reconnected a few years back. On a rainy afternoon, while Naeto was preparing for his third-year seminar, Gozi had sent him a congratulatory email for his many achievements. Naeto had stopped everything. That one-paragraph text was all that mattered. Only Gozi would rejoin society and send a text via email. The boys emailed every day, talking about the most random things: the first time they tried lasagna, and how toilet paper was getting softer. They talked about River. And when Gozi mentioned he had moved back home, Naeto went home too.

With his luggage and all, Naeto had his haxi hover straight to Gozi's old house. The house was still there, though the compound looked different. Gozi's moms had been farmers, and their home had been a haven for all growing and crawling things. Having returned a few months earlier, Gozi had taken things a step further. Their home was now a sanctuary. And there was the color, like the rains of April came and never left. Green moss, like green carpets, crawled over the house and barn in the most deliberate manner. Vines, branches, and foliage looped and weaved down the roof, down the wooden pillars. There were trees everywhere, and the breeze whistled through the leaves, and like a hall of children, they whispered. Surrounding the compound, fallow land stretched forth, dotted with wildflowers, and the sun danced on their petals. And what followed the color was the sound, the soft, gentle call of animals breathing. Every step Naeto took sent grasshoppers darting off the thigh-high grass. The rabbits followed, peeping cautiously before scurrying into the underbrush. Above, squirrels and sparrows chattered in the trees. A herd of sheep cut in front of him, their wool, a billowing black. In a corner laid a Great Pyrenees, a quiet sentry on guard.

Naeto followed the sound of wood being chopped. He followed it past some goats scaling the low walls. He followed it past gobbling turkeys and clucking hens. And he found Gozi. This Gozi was many things. He was bigger, taller. With each measured swing, his arms bulged like ukwa pods. His shoulders were as broad as doors. Sweat gleamed down his forehead, streaming onto the log below. Gozi was a big, bearded man chopping wood. His axe came down again, and steel met wood, and what was one log became two.

And Gozi saw him.

Of course Naeto wasn't going to run away. He was not twelve anymore. Still, he considered it.

"Hey." He waved with both his hands. *Why did he do that? One hand would have been sufficient!*

Gozi said nothing. He looked at Naeto like he was seeing him for the first time. The big man's stare was steel. Then, in one motion, he dropped the axe, rushed up to Naeto, and embraced him, lifting him slightly off the floor. His sweat and dirt were now on Naeto like they had been there all along. Unsure but slowly, Naeto embraced his friend back. And for a moment, they were twelve again, tinkering with things they shouldn't tinker with.

"You're . . . " Naeto gestured at all of him, " . . . bigger."

Gozi smiled, his cedar-brown eyes crinkling at the corners. "And you're still you."

But so was Gozi. He had tripled in size, morphed, and shifted in the passing years, but his face was still his face, and his eyes were still his. There were other things. Gozi had lost a leg after the accident, after they had found him unconscious by the lake. He now had a prosthetic one. Naeto knew about this.

"I—ehm—I wanted to say—" Naeto started.

"It doesn't matter anymore." Gozi softly shook his head.

And the two friends sat, and talked, and remembered everything. They remembered River. And as they remembered, it was like they had never been separated all those years ago. Like they were not reuniting twelve years later. Like they were just two friends hanging out like they did every other day.

"Will I see you again tomorrow?"

"Yes. Yes."

They saw each other the next day, the day after that, and the day after. One evening, Gozi took Naeto down to the lake, and there it was—River's canoe.

"All this time." Naeto ran his hands along its rough exterior.

River completed it before she left their sector. Two years later, she built another canoe in Seattle and sailed into a river. It was the last time she was seen.

"I want to show you something." Gozi climbed into the canoe and stretched his hand to Naeto.

Naeto took his hand.

The boys rowed River's canoe into the lake, and it skimmed the waters like it belonged there. The reeds welcomed them, nodding in the delicate breeze. The water was more crystal than Naeto remembered. Through the floating flora, he could see the scales on the tilapia and the smooth corners of the pebbles at the bottom. The canoe's paddles were mismatched pairs of oars. In their design was River's impatience, but also her will. When the paddles parted the water, Naeto felt the lake in his arms. It was strong but not tethering, a gentle tug, like friends holding hands, like water finding water. Small pools of lake water gathered at their feet, but the vessel was not built to sink. A small current came, and the canoe creaked, the canoe bent. Naeto did not waver—for bending was not breaking. He knew River's canoe would steady.

And the canoe sailed, like a dream half-realized, but a dream, nonetheless.

They reached the other side of the lake, to a field that stretched for miles. Naeto never knew about this field.

"Gozi, what are we doing here?"

"Just wait. You'll see."

The two friends sat in the tall, tall grass, waiting, watching the sunset. Then they laid in the grass. Soon, the sun lowered behind a forested hill, giving way to the moon.

"It's time." Gozi stood.

"Time for what?" Naeto came up too, trying to find his friend in the darkness.

Gozi took Naeto's face in his cold palms, turning it away from his, and towards the empty distance. "Just wait."

Naeto waited, his eyes finding the night, his feet sinking slightly into the mellow soil, his breathing clear in his ears. Gozi's breathing found his, blending into his. And Naeto waited, and waited, and he saw.

It was one speck. Soft and aglow. Light becoming. It sailed, higher, higher. One firefly against the night. And what was one became two, and what was two became ten thousand, as waves of fireflies lifted from the grass like lanterns, their wings; silk whispering to silk. And all the fireflies reached for heaven, beginning where the stars ended.

Their glow, a thing unbroken, a thing afire, touched all the corners of Naeto's face. They touched his glasses, and Naeto saw light.

Naeto held a gasp, soft laughter and tears escaping him. The fireflies were as farlights finding each other. Slowly, he reached out, his hand sailing higher, higher, pinpricks of light finding his skin, illuminating him, and Naeto touched infinity.

"When did they come back?"

"I don't know. I came, and they were here." Standing side by side, Gozi snuck his hand into Naeto's, one shy finger at a time. "They are here because of you. Because of the River Naetozi Tinker lights. It worked, like you said it would."

"I—I did it for you."

It felt like they were back in Gozi's bedroom all those years ago. Naeto looked away, reaching for his glasses. They did not need cleaning. And Gozi led his hands away from them. He took Naeto's face, eyes finding eyes, and kissed him. A gentle thing. And Naeto did not run away.

ABOUT THE AUTHOR

Somto Ihezue (he/him) is a Nigerian-Igbo writer, editor, and filmmaker. He is a creative writing MFA student at the University of Maryland, and is a scholarship recipient from Clarion West, Tin House, Voodoonauts, and Milford SF workshops. His works have appeared, or are forthcoming at *Tor, The Magazine of Fantasy & Science Fiction, Uncanny, Strange Horizons, Nightmare, Beneath Ceaseless Skies, PodCastle, Escape Pod, PseudoPod, Poetry Magazine,* and others. His stories have been shortlisted for the British Fantasy (Sydney J. Bounds), Nommo, and Utopia Awards. As an anthologist, his work includes *Publishing Taught Me* (as assistant editor) and *Will This Be A Problem?* (as co-editor).

A Planet Full of Sorrows
M. L. CLARK

Everyone on the *Ember* dreams of Emanuel.

Case says he's always lippy with her in dreams, and that she's had it up to here with his post-mortem attitude, but none of us is buying the complaint. Emanuel and Case always had the flirty rapport of a young man who prefers men and an older woman who prefers women, and after eight sols together under contract, Emanuel's sass and Case's sass-back were as close as any of us ever came to an "I love you" on our mess of a deep-space crew.

Meanwhile, Riviera says Emanuel will drift by her bunk while she dreams of working the engines—*and don't you go judging my dreams now; I'll dream of power couplers as much as I like*—then tell her things about the universe. What things, we'll ask her. Oh, just things, she'll say. Sometimes where the last packet of vintage was hiding. Sometimes prophetic visions about the ship, the system, and us. Once, Emanuel told her the exact day the last settlement on Old Earth would die out, though she refuses to tell us when that is.

"What difference would it make?" she says. "What any of *you* gon' do about it?"

Hiraj dreams of the accident itself, which makes sense since he was there. Hiraj dreams of running in spot on the outer hull, mag-boots and boosters ever-failing as he tries to reach our flight specialist out on repairs. It should have been a minor incident, a simple misstep after Emanuel's line caught on a twist of damaged paneling and he stumbled, but as Emanuel's body jerked toward the ship, his helmet struck some of the scarred, jagged metal along the hull—a fluke blow, entirely preventable—and then . . . just like that.

A whole universe could and did end so easily.

When I dream of Emanuel he talks to me, but I can't understand a word he's saying—which is curious, because I've been a good lip-reader for years, ever since my hearing started to go. A cranial implant helps me follow the crew's speech on the *Ember*, and haptics in my suit pick up more sounds around me on walkabout, but in my dreams Emanuel and I are in the mess together, I guess shooting the updraft from how relaxed he always looks, and yet . . . nothing. His lips move, he smiles at me, he gestures with his hands, but not a thing he does translates in my mind to language. For a comms specialist, it's maddening.

But maybe that's the point.

Maybe we all dream of Emanuel as a reminder of the limits to what we can ever do, or prevent, or know. Maybe he keeps coming back to us, four cycles after his passing, because we're all holding on to something bigger than we should, and he's trying to tell us . . .

Let go, you old space bums.

Let go.

"Rom! Rom! You can't just switch off the network like that. You . . . of all of us . . . need to stay . . . in contact . . . all the time!"

I listen as Hiraj stops to catch his breath. We're close enough that I'm catching his shouts through sensors along the back of my suit, which aren't perfect—tons of distortion, leaving my mind to fill in the blanks—but that's fine by me. I'm avoiding the greater network for now, and make no apology for it. Yes, I feel sorry for worrying my oldest friend, my last binding tie to an overrun world many sols from here, but not enough to cater to his hyperbolic fears. My location and vitals were never offline, our suits are pinging back and forth, and Riv and Case up in orbit always have eyes on us. I just have main comms off while I work.

And more importantly, while I *think*, which sometimes involves muttering aloud.

These days, anything you utter on comms is as good as stored forever, you know?

If Emanuel were here, mind you, he'd knock insistently on my helmet, laugh, and ask me who the hell I was talking to—whether I muttered aloud or not. He could always tell.

"Is that God in there with you?" he'd tease. "Or El Diablo?"

It's common for spacers to talk to themselves—or to the ether, or to a bunch of little ghosts inside their heads that vaguely remind them of people they once knew—but in this case, it's more than that. I think I'm trying to explain to myself why I'm still alive.

Why me, and not him.

Why now, and why here.

Why did *we* have to be the ones to find this place?

Why did anyone?

Why couldn't it have remained obscure, untouched, forever?

Why did I have to leave Clorus-5?

Why couldn't I be dozing right now in the shade of the family's grazing cattle, on a ranch where my parents' generation hybridized the local wildlife using a grant and special resources from Interplanetary, with nothing but a clean wash of pink-orange skies above me, and the faint sound of community chatter on the comms helmet buzzing at my side?

Hiraj doesn't even attempt to join me on the stone ledge where I'm holo-sketching the surrounding vista, deep in the jungles of the planet Alaru. It's a bit of a steep climb, and not all of us take as well to heavy grav after long stints on the *Ember*, where some of us (let's face it) have been pretty lax when it comes to routine muscle training. Hell, Case couldn't come planetside for anything over 0.8-Standard if she wanted to anymore, though she'd be the first to tell you that she wouldn't want to be down here anyway—or on any terrestrial port. The illusion of gravity created by the ship's habitat ring, emulating a decent 0.4-S, is as close as she gets to the pull of the stuff, and she's been known to side-eye even that from time to time.

The reason for our presence looms unevenly in the distance: an ancient, pristine city in the middle of a dense, muggy forest on a lone continent. A vast mist shrouds the bulk of this urban intrusion, but from my vantage point you can still make out monuments in profile, at varying depths, which is precisely why I climbed up here to record what I could: to get a feel for the place from another perspective. To sneak up on any greater meaning from behind.

Before me, under the nearby mist line, long corridors of dark, glinting pillars mark out a labyrinth of residential zones around a hexagonal center, one side of which opens into a massive crypt. Occupied, of course—but not by humans.

Aliens: very dead, very un-human, and very much not local.

This isn't our planet, and it wasn't theirs, either, but you don't get to be picky when it comes to first contact with a high-sentient species. Oh, sure, Emanuel would've been furious to see this, but only as an affect. He would have grown theatrically pissy to lighten the mood for the rest of us, once we realized what we'd stumbled upon, and while we were busy trying to process the bigger implications of everything we said or did after that point. What was the first word one of us said, when we saw those massive tombs? Pretty sure it wasn't anything pithy—probably on the level of "oh fuck!" or "nobody shit themselves!" Words for the history vids.

But Emanuel . . . Emanuel had a gift for such things.

While the rest of us were scanning for life signs and taking readings of the scale and complexity of surrounding structures, he would have started complaining about something inconsequential or outright absurd. The lack of amenities in the abandoned city, maybe.

I could imagine him running into the center of the city, his arms thrown wide as he spun around to take in the shockingly immaculate whole of the place.

What, all this and no room service?

He'd said it often enough when sent out on the *Ember*'s solar skiff for recon, repair, or resource-gathering missions, as a way of shaking off any creeping claustrophobia before it had a chance to sink in. And then—

Boy, when did your ass ever make enough chit for room service? Riv would fire back.

Riviera could always call him "boy".

Case, not so much.

You'd better not nick the towels and good soaps while you're in there, she'd shoot through comms instead—though when she'd last had anything beyond a sonic scouring was anyone's guess. Some things we carry with us from our terrestrial starts, even after all this time in the stars. Hiraj and me, from Clorus-5. Emanuel, from Buendia-4. Case from New Oslo, home of Interplanetary headquarters. Riv from Old Earth—but don't ask from where exactly on it, if you don't want your head half bitten off.

That back-and-forth had been our ship's little ritual against dying—or against worrying about death, at least—whenever Emanuel crammed himself into that tight little space for the multiple shifts it might take to see the skiff safely home. And we could've used a taste of that ritual the first time we set foot in the alien city, before we realized that the only other extraterrestrials on Alaru were all dead and at rest in massive, crystalline structures. None of us thought we were going to die there, too, exactly, but there was a clear sense of having stepped into a different reality—a universe where highly sentient aliens were fact, not vid-fodder; and where humanity was just a little less consequential because of it.

What's a body supposed to do, or feel, when the switch flips on everything they'd taken for granted? We were all bracing for the next big shift in reality. In those first few hours, while we moved through row upon row of alien dead, multidimensional monsters could have burst from thin air and we would've freaked out on sight, sure, but also thought to ourselves . . .

Yeah, okay, all things considering . . . that tracks.

We survived that first day on Alaru, though.

Even without Emanuel's humor by our side.

And yet, why wouldn't we? The sheer age of this abandoned city, buried in the middle of a giant continent rich with floral, fungal, insect, and reptilian life that came to a sudden halt at the perimeter of the alien structure, suggests that we missed our high-sentient associates by centuries. Maybe a millennium. For all we know, the rest of their kind is now extinct, and maybe has been for hundreds of sols. Maybe they enjoyed their brief, furious window of exploration and adventure-seeking, then died off, killed by a mix of hubris and bureaucracy.

Won't be the last time, if so—but why go into that with the little people in my head, watching in? Even mere ghosts in my mind's eye have surely seen all the reports and forum posts freaking out over the decline of humanity's once-proud mining and homesteader projects. Scathing remarks about corporate takeovers on rugged little outposts started by brave communalists with a dream and a drive. The story, maybe, of my own Clorus-5, which these days I hear has just the ugliest range of industrial grays up on high.

Ghosts like you don't need a rehash of the basics simply to pass judgment on what I'm doing here, but maybe some of the latest mods from Interplanetary haven't found their way to every corner of the galaxy yet, and you're not aware of everything we can do now. Maybe ghosts like you never bothered with holo-sketch programs like my AugMind, which feeds info from my suit's external sensors through algorithms relentlessly tweaked by science teams across Interplanetary, to fill in the blanks my eyes couldn't reach even in better seasons of my life. I tell the program where and how to focus on the ancient city from my stony perch, and it enhances the scans my suit picks up, adding details about chemical composition, biological components, age, radioactivity, and stability for the structures below—no guesswork, just a powerful, on-the-spot synthesis of suit data. It's a useful symbiosis, if also less a choice and more an imperative as my personal sensory "equipment" starts to fade. First the hearing, now my eyesight—plus two fingers of my left hand that can't ever seem to keep still.

I remind myself that Hiraj is trying to be a useful symbiote, too.

Emanuel isn't with us anymore, but Hiraj is—just as he's been for me since we first put our parents on Clorus-5 on secure migrant ships, then pulled a pair of choice Interplanetary contracts and started hitching rides of our own with far-off exploration crews.

"We need you," he says again. "—with comms on . . . all the time!"

The words still come to me as vibrations, and from their diffuse nature I can tell he's shouting even louder now to bridge the distance. It reminds me of a time when we had to get all the livestock in during an electrical storm, and we were out waving and shouting at each other through a dangerous crackle in the air that made the use of any electronics suspect. Back then, though, there had been animals bolting hard and in circles between us, bleating and bucking and ready to knock us over with the winds rising. Now *that* was danger.

This? Two old farts a few meters off in a fairly sedate jungle: a few venomous lizards and corrosive fungal species aside? This is nothing.

Still, I hear my old friend's underlying bid for reassurance, and I defer to it in spirit, while tidying up a few lines on my holo-sketch. Hiraj will be drenched with sweat inside his own suit by now, after all that running in this muggy heat. The temptation to tear off his helmet must be so strong, especially since we all know the atmosphere here is good.

Better than good, actually. On arrival, a yellow-orange glow off Alaru's ionosphere hinted at an atmosphere rich in oxygen and nitrogen, initially promising an easy planet to claim and prep for settlements on Interplanetary's behalf. And what a sweet little payday this would have been, if so—with plenty of flora and fauna that could be hybridized to serve new arrivals' needs. Hell, we could have switched off the discovery forums, with all their ship-to-ship soap-operas and dishonest private postings, and coasted in our grief for a few cycles before taking on any new assignments . . . *if* Alaru had been as simple as a Class-IV world should be.

But no such luck—and no such hope for internal calm, which is part of why the helmet stays on until long-term field tests are completed. Ever since Emanuel's freak accident, our team's been sticklers for the rules, and the presence of non-native aliens doesn't help: who knows what pathogens might've been created when the biochem from two worlds collided?

Oh, our crew's grief-caution will probably wear off in a few more cycles, but for now, on the *Ember*, it's all doting, heavy-handed care for each other.

And it's smothering, really.

Almost as smothering as the jungle heat.

I make sure Hiraj is looking at me when I sign at him, *This can't all be on record.*

He looks confused. Then his shoulders slump. The scientist in him understands before the rest: he's remembering my frustration over what happened to my first field report, and how someone on Interplanetary's "civilian" council leaked the classified document to those damned forums. His own hand signs are rough, but they get the job done.

CAN'T—LOSE YOU—TOO. CAPTAIN—PLATE—ENOUGH.

It's funny how some figurative speech outlives its context. I try to remember the last time Case, or any of us, ate from an actual plate: not a tray, bag, or squeeze-packet.

I'm not gone. I'm right here! But even as my irritation rises with Hiraj, I know there's nothing fair about my attitude. It's not his fault that he didn't see what I did on our first visit to the city. And it's not his fault that he hasn't been back since. I mean, *maybe* it's his fault, technically, but he's had plenty of other survey work to do elsewhere in the region. Just because there's this massive alien structure plunked straight in the middle of an alien world doesn't mean the other elements here aren't worth studying—especially to a xenobiologist eager to pre-empt a classic terraforming team field report.

I will myself calm before adding:

Do you want to see them?

Hiraj goes back to shouting, my suit picking up trace vibrations. "See what?"

I let my hands fall slack beside me and wait until he's ready to listen.

If my suit's network were switched on, I'm sure I'd hear him panting through comms, trying to get his bearings this deep in the jungle—and so close to nightfall, with shadow upon shadow doing nothing for the heat but everything for tricks of the mind. As it is, all I see is his suit heaving a little, like he's still working on self-control.

FINE. YES. SHOW ME.

I flash a thumbs up and switch off the holo-sketch program before hopping down. Hiraj startles, but once I'm up close I see wary trust though the round of his helmet glass, and I clap his shoulder, clinging to that thin thread of confidence.

I know what he's telling himself. He's telling himself,

Rom's a reliable guy who knows his stuff. If he says there are ghosts in the ruins, he doesn't mean it like folklore. He's talking about something we can quantify. He hasn't lost his damned mind.

I'm embellishing, obviously, but that last part is what I see in Hiraj's eyes when I get close: a conviction that my old friend needs to hold so he can trust and follow me, when . . .

Honestly?

Honestly, I have no idea if he really should.

I'm still not sure what to believe myself.

From up on the *Ember* for the last few shifts, Case and Riviera have been feeding us updates about the space race of fanatics rushing toward Alaru since our report was leaked. We all knew it had to have been done on purpose. Last year—you remember, right?—there was that bitter election of a major figure from private industry: someone who'd been trying to get his claws into the public trust of Interplanetary forever, and who finally got a loophole to work in his favor. So who could be surprised when, mere months after Eskin became chair, one of the most important classified reports for the future of deep-space discovery got loose a week after its submission, and whipped up all kinds of private enterprise eager to reach Alaru first?

The fact that Eskin had deep ties to the orthodox fetishists, the prophets, *and* the exorcists—our three front-runners in evangelical space exploration, though you probably know them better by the ridiculous names of their missions (which I and the rest of the *Ember*'s crew refuse to use: don't get us started on how frustrating it is to see all the forums take them seriously)—was also no great shock. There are no laws saying Eskin can't pay religious tribute, even to organizations that then use his donation to buy tons of transport tech *from* him—from that vast, shady empire developed well outside Interplanetary purview.

And what happens when there's a lot of business flowing into a company, even if the exchanges are ultimately recycling Eskin's own money? Suddenly others want to invest, too. So any fool with eyes—even ones losing their luster, like mine—can tell you that Eskin wins no matter which religious group reaches Alaru first. All that matters for his status and profit margin is that a race is on at all, to keep public and private interest in his products competitive.

Less easy to predict, if you ask me, was what *exactly* about our preliminary report would make everyone go space-mad. I mean, we'd found a whole alien city dropped in the middle of another world, filled with tombs of their mysterious dead, and no other signs of them on a planet just about optimal for human settlement.

You'd think that would be enough!

But no. Humans are too fickle, I guess. We're always looking for some special new angle, and so it was a few bloody words in my section of the initial report, commenting on something I'd seen during my first passage into the mist, that consumed everyone's imaginations and launched a thousand or so nutbags on their Eskin-derived mission ships.

"Ghost-like quality," I'd written. "A figure in the dark?"

Yeah, that was all on me. I should have stuck to hard, observable facts. It doesn't matter that what I saw more or less lined up with the crystalline dead we found soon after, and there were so many explanations we hadn't ruled out by the time we filed that report. It was irresponsible of me to let that indulgent first impression linger in the report's final form.

And yet, I hadn't thought much of it, at first. It was a classified document. It was supposed to be read by scientists and other civic representatives who took their jobs seriously and understood that the future of space expansion was in their hands.

In the end, I'd trusted too much in the resilience of Interplanetary networks to shelter human error from the whims of private enterprise. Like Emanuel out on repairs, cracking his damned helmet on a rogue twist of damaged metal, I'd grown too comfortable with the old lay of the land, even when there were obvious signs of how much had been transformed.

Ah . . . but what's to be done about it now?

When it comes to care in new environments, out on the hull or in the jaws of public-private bureaucracy, all we can ever do is try to mind our safety protocols a little better; and in my case, watch whatever the hell else I say—out loud, at least—now that I know it might end up in the wrong hands.

Oh, and wait, as it turns out.

Waiting's been a big part of our last few weeks on Alaru—and yes, it's been driving us mad. We're used to holding down the fort on a new world, but for archaeologists or xenobiologists, or terraform engineers to survey the local geochem.

You know, any of the usual teams Interplanetary launches after a xenobiological find.

Instead, Hiraj and I were surface-side when Case and Riv relayed word of the space race that had won out instead: a tight council vote ultimately decided in favor of the "delicate existential nature of this find." We could hardly believe it—the bald-faced commercialism of it all—even though each of us had a hard-luck story of being driven from our first homes once private enterprise saw something they liked in settlements initially built by collective trust, under the guidance of Interplanetary governance. Our captain and lead engineer were glued to their feeds for hours after that stunning announcement, boggling at the range of promo campaigns helping major and minor players compete for the stars.

"So, who's gonna make it here first, you think?" Case had asked, after we all had a go at swearing profusely over how far Interplanetary had fallen. "The exorcists or the prophets?"

But Riv beat us to an answer, in part because Hiraj and I were still recovering from the heat in our base-camp bunks. "Say we get lucky," she'd said. "Then it's the Orthodox fetishists. You know they've already got a solid franchise goin'—temple experiences all up and down the galactic arm. And when you add alien bodies and ghosts and shit to the mix? Baby, now you're talkin' a crown jewel for the whole chain."

"And they're the best option because . . . ?" Hiraj had asked around a yawn.

"They're just after profit," said Case. "And they don't even try to hide it. Yeah, Riv, I think you're on to something. If the fetishists get here first, Interplanetary can cut a deal. If all they really want is a place to set up shop and tell stories, maybe the council can give them part of the yellow moon and apply their payoff to fund archaeology on the surface."

I'd snorted. "Like the council under Eskin won't try to sell them a lot more. You know he's already got another home in mind for all the chit he's making personally by promising to parcel out Alaru through Interplanetary."

More cussing filled the *Ember* at his name, and at the games we all knew were being played. At the time, I'd wondered if Case and Riviera had put the ship's systems on semi-auto and got into the vintage. Alcohol was too dangerous for space—at least, if you wanted your ship's water reclamation systems to work properly—but there were some fine market alternatives that delivered a mild buzz a stim patch could quickly counter in the case of a crisis.

But when the swearing eased—or at least, when we'd come to a natural lull while rooting around for more inventive turns of phrase to describe the disaster back in HQ—Riv took my side, sighing heavily.

"Ah, well, for sure you know that's right, Rom. When it comes to sellin' out, there's no way around it, council as it is. Once they set up license agreements for different access tiers, we can all say kiss-kiss adios to any science surface-side. Still," she'd sniffed, her gaze drifting as if she'd just heard someone speaking to her from the empty corridor. "Better than the alternative, hey? Can't pay off exorcists."

Hiraj mumbled something, then repeated it louder when Case told him to give the old crones on *Ember* a break with his whispers. I'd almost snorted at the time: as if either Case or Riviera were as old as me and Hiraj, or falling apart even half as much!

"I said, 'not that they aren't profit-driven, too'!"

"Well, yeah," said Case, after a pause. "But the exorcists get their profit through back-end investors who pull the strings and get first dibs on spoils from the mess they leave behind. We're talking about the kind of crazies that made a whole industry out of purging settlements of supposed spooks and demons—and not because the settlements were paying to be wiped out!"

Put that way, it occurred to me then: there wasn't much difference between what exorcists did to settlements unfortunate enough to draw their notice, and what other private organizations did to places like Clorus-5. Exorcists simply did with grand, mythic shows what other grifters did by "summoning the spirit" of the free market. And when those fanatics were finished casting demons out (and decent residents with them), whatever abandoned properties remained would be perfect to sell to scavengers—just like the corporate enterprise that had swept through my father's farm, and Hiraj's mother's: promising everyone on the settlement a better life, only to sell off their life's work for parts.

That first night, while venting over the space race, I'd hummed in agreement, then spoken louder than I thought was necessary, just in case. "Plus, on all those other worlds, the biggest aliens were shrubs and insects. This is huge. This is way more than an investment opportunity: it's a challenge. I wouldn't be surprised if they're already claiming the Devil lives on Alaru. They're going to milk this exorcism for everything they can."

Two groans came down the line, concurring. I glanced at Hiraj on the opposite bunk, and we smiled wearily at each other amid Case and Riv's next round of chatter. I knew what we were both thinking, amid all that evening's griping over things we couldn't change:

Emanuel would've loved this.

Emanuel should still have been alive, to cuss out Eskin's name with us, too.

I guide Hiraj to the city of the dead, taking my time on account of his clear exhaustion. It's our second trip together, though I've been back plenty while Hiraj was doing his botanical and animal-studies thing. The last time I'd seen him this reluctant to visit a haunted place, displacement orders had just come through for our folks, and he never wanted to set foot on his mother's homestead again. He wouldn't tell me directly, though—just always had excuses to steer clear, while I helped her and my father prep for the evac shuttle. I figured Hiraj wasn't great at goodbyes, or much inclined to "take a good look" for posterity's sake.

Might be that's why he can't stop dreaming of trying to rescue Emanuel, either.

He was *there* when something he loved got taken down, and he's never been the type to be *there* without wanting to do something about it.

This is probably also why he's been so damned annoying around me lately—brotherly, even: trying to make up for a body of grieving put off for too long.

We both loved him, and we all miss him. I would've told Hiraj if he ever opened up about it. But then again, when had I? I didn't hear so well anymore, but I could speak, couldn't I? And to something other than the ghosts inside my head?

Well, but maybe not. While Emanuel was alive, we'd cared too much about each other to cross the line. All these sols together, our youngest member had enlivened the whole crew's hearts—but complexly, through many wavelengths of love and longing at once—so who among us was ever going to mess with a good thing by throwing in a question, a proposition, a new dynamic that risked throwing all five of us off course?

We aren't exactly silent as we descend, me and Hiraj. My suit picks up and amplifies every crunch and snap of foliage as we approach a wide recess in the forest before the main alien infrastructure begins. I know adjustments had to be made for my loss of hearing, but it's uncanny, recognizing a vibration along one's spacesuit as echolocated sounds from someone nearby. Sometimes, when I'm half-asleep or drifting aboard the *Ember*, I lose track of a limb or can't sense exactly where my fingers are, but out in these suits it's like I'm wrapped in one big sensory amplifier. Every little bit of external input feels like it's sharpening the borders of where "I" begin and end . . . and yet, also somehow doing the opposite, making me feel larger than myself. More connected with everything around me.

It's as though the ends of me stretch out into the jungle: as if I'm bound by the suit *to* Hiraj, and to every living thing around him. Around us. The "ghost-like quality" of his movements traces itself along the haptics on my back. I feel the trees there, too, and insect song, and what I can only describe as background heat, lapping at my sensors.

Suffocating, spiritual, or both?

The recess that runs through this stretch of Alaru's wildlife, starting at a little green stream and moving gently toward the city, is a curious thing, out in the middle of a sprawling jungle that should have overrun it centuries ago. It doesn't seem to have been designed as an entrance. It features no grand arches, no art or labels, and no clear way of closing it off in an emergency. But the intentionality can be seen in how surrounding flora comes close to the path, then arcs around it: a long sequence of circle-segments bordering us on either side, suggesting a series of objects embedded in the rocks beneath us to keep Alaru out, even after all this time. My suit picks up heat, but no more dangerous radiation than the rest of the wilds contain. At best, it has the feel of an emergency evac-route, established by beings who had no idea that it would one day help other aliens walk right in.

Except that there are no flatlands on the other end—so how would they have evacuated? To what nearby haven would they have escaped?

We'd seen no signs of dump sites, mines, or storage beyond city limits, let alone anything resembling a landing site. But then, we were coming late to the question—hundreds of years late—and Alaru is a dynamic planet, richly alive and more than capable of growing over even major clues. If a proper field team is ever allowed to do its work here, it might discover all sorts of alien artifacts embedded in the flora, or the stones. But all hope of grand discoveries will fade the moment that any of those fanatics land. At best, maybe a missionary will find and pocket scraps of alien material, to show up later in a shrine or alt-market on the forums. Meanwhile, all subtler signs of this ancient civilization, like this offhand route around the city's limits, will be trampled in a heartbeat.

I can just imagine the "history" vids that fanatics will make when they get here, too. Soon discovery forums will boast dozens of broadcasts of deranged prophets clutching alien skulls and waving theatrically at the rest of the crypt while filling in the blanks, telling tall tales about who these creatures were and what they were doing here.

Shit. They'll probably even get to *name* them. Nothing catchy has landed yet in the forums, but it's only a matter of time, and maybe a little marketing. Soon we'll have cartoon versions of Alaru aliens on packets of vintage and fuel bars, and a whole new industry of vid-games imagining a coming war where we have to blast them to pieces.

Civilization!

What a great idea.

We should look into it.

As Hiraj and I advance toward the city, the jungle darkens less from a lack of daylight and more from the immensity of rocks replacing flora around us. Eventually we reach a thin ground-level haze, which marks the presence of a still-active sensor system that seems harmless to us, but keeps other critters from wandering in. Even mighty tree roots that have broken through surrounding rock formations take the hint when they reach this point, and grow in other directions, their heavy black limbs twisting sharply and doubling over in retreat.

Hallowed ground?

Or a fine-tuned set of interactions between the mist system and local biochemistry?

I take a beat to entertain a wicked fantasy: the exorcists burning up on entry here, or—even better—crashing into Alaru's massive ocean, never to be heard from again. But when have the fates ever been so kind? I skip ahead, diving straight into the gray.

Once I've descended into the city's depths, I lose all sense of Hiraj—no more heavy vibrations at my back, through the suit—so I switch on my local channel and look back. All I can see are Hiraj's boots beneath the irradiating haze, planted firmly at a higher point on the downward sloping stones. I wait for him to descend as I have, but all I see is flecks of jungle mud fall free from his boots and disintegrate in the mist.

It's quiet down here, too. I've lost all sense again of where I begin and end.

"You're like Jiffy, you know that?"

Hiraj's boots wobble in place; I've startled him with my sudden switch to comms. A mean trick, the sort we used to play as kids, a million sols ago.

"Your dad's horse?"

"The same."

I wonder what I look like from his vantage point, as he watches me from above the mist. Probably "ghost-like": my weary body consumed by this sea of shadows, a darker shade among shades, dwarfed by massive stone structures.

Possibly, my reference feels like a haunting to him, too, because I've invoked a story from an entirely different world—a planet of heat and desert, and flora that only blooms at night—and from a whole other era in our lives. A time before economic attrition drove all the youth from our settlement, and before our parents and grandparents were packed up and shuttled off to another Interplanetary base. A time before private industry moved in and priced out what was supposed to be a world without all the corporate nonsense of the rest.

"When Jiffy was a colt," I continue, "he got spooked at this one turn on the back route across the ranch. There was some snake or lizard zipping across the path, Dad said. Fluke event. Could've been anything. But every time we took him out after, he'd always tense up at that same spot. Not at any other spot where he'd ever seen a snake—but that first one, right out of the corral? It always got to him, right until the day he died."

Hiraj grunts, and through comms the sound reverberates. He gets my point. He's frozen right where I first saw the anomaly I mentioned in my report, along one of the first pillars that form a long chain toward the city's hexagonal center. Hiraj didn't see it himself back then, but knowing this is where it happened for me must've spooked him all the same.

Plus, there's something about *this* spot, the obvious symbolism of descending into the unknown and being met by an unknown there, that would rattle anyone. That's why I always dive in: I don't want to give myself the chance to dwell on superstition longer than I must.

"This way," I say. "I won't wait for you forever. And then what'll you tell Case, if you lose me in the mist?" I switch off the channel and press on.

But I glance back as I move, in time to see him take a few more unsteady steps into the mist, only regaining his resolve once he's entirely through. Together, single-file, we walk into the heart of the alien compound. The terrain is almost disappointingly quiet as we pass between two dark, highly polished red-brown columns (garnet, we've assessed, though the crystal is infused with other metals, too) and enter a series of labyrinthine corridors that always annoy me at first sight, for multiple reasons.

The first has to do with the city's impeccable cleanliness, ill-suited to its eons-old status. That lack of filth speaks to a system set up to keep the joint immaculate—something in the mist, maybe, considering how easily it knocked mud off Hiraj's boots—but what's the point of keeping this place so damned clean for so damned long, if its inhabitants aren't ever coming back? If they're all dead in their crystal tombs?

Or was the cleaning of the columns incidental? A side-effect of something the mist did for the aliens, while they were first setting up camp in the middle of another world? I can almost forgive the aggravatingly immaculate state of this place when I imagine our predecessors as even half as neurotic as we humans are, with all our safety protocols that always feel a touch excessive, right until they end up saving untold numbers of foolish lives.

Emanuel would've loved that image, too. Germophobic xenomorphs!

Then there's the second issue: the frustrating schism between advancement and simplicity in the whole urban design. The city's perimeter system makes abundantly clear that we're dealing with a highly developed civilization, as does the very fact of the species' settlement on a whole other world. And yet, everything about the infrastructure lacks signs of higher computing, data storage, and language in general. How did these aliens communicate? Where did they keep their need-to-knows? Even their ancient households are like every flattened, stereotypical performance of alien life you've ever seen in low-budget holo-vids: mere aesthetic backdrop, absent any sign of everyday routines, let alone marks of individual character or domestic variation from one dwelling to the next. Where did they take out their trash? Where did they gather casually between work tasks? What were their vices and crutches?

There are no obvious machine interfaces, either. No markings on the wall or indications of material culture in any of the chambers. No hints of star charts on the ceilings. No clear cultural coding to the patterns on the floors. No memorial plaques even in the main resting place, and none of the paraphernalia found in any resting place ever seen on human-settled worlds. There are no signs of tribute, and no obvious signs of hierarchy for the dead.

And yet, even from the absence of material artifacts, there's plenty for a forensic investigator to learn from a site like this: far more than the AugMind program can intuit from my limited wanderings here, certainly.

For one, this species clearly believes (or believed) in the value of preservation, because all the alien bodies have been crystallized in fetal poses that scans suggest are a natural state, rather than the result of post-mortem repositioning.

They're also not adorned with any clothes or trinkets: a sign that should have made it easy to conclude that this culture doesn't believe in an afterlife where one might need items from this one, except . . . well, the crypt itself resembles the surrounding city, with each dead alien more or less situated in a space that maps easily onto many of the residential quarters in the city at large. Does that count as imagining life after death?

Maybe the whole culture just likes to keep things minimal, but if so, what does this tell us about their cosmology? Their sense of purpose? Were they warriors who prided themselves on abstaining from the usual spectacle of battle finery and trophies? Or humble workers in hive-clusters, for whom the concept of owning personal items would have baffled all involved?

And either way, why set up this city where they did, dead-center in a massive jungle on Alaru's lone continent? Not even the yellow moon in this planet's sky boasts other signs of alien presence—or any signs of life at all. Beyond the little recess we use to enter the main compound, our predecessors here seem to have arrived solely to embed their structure on the surface, then depart. Scared away, the job half-finished? What job, if so?

Or maybe the point was exactly what it looks like: to deposit their dead in a mausoleum of a city, which only exists to serve as a massive monument to their lives. That would certainly explain why each dead alien matches a specific residential plot. Maybe these aliens were so far-reaching in their empire that they could indulge in using whole worlds for mere flyby tributes. Could the whole structure be a memorial—even the parts well outside the tombs?

Hiraj comes to a halt beside me, after I've stopped in the middle of the hexagonal commons and pointed to one of the corridors on the far side of the city-center. Hiraj's gaze follows the path of my outstretched hand, then leaps beyond it, toward the pillars of darkly glinting garnet furthest from us. He grips my other arm tightly. "What the—"

I bring my hand to the front of his helmet, a finger raised. *Shh.*

Hiraj steadies himself and stares at the phantom form in the shadowy walkway. It's just a trace of a figure. A smudge in the haze. But while it's there, it's a three-meters-tall wanderer in these ancient, empty, near-pristine city grounds.

It has a cloak-like skin-flap fused to two massive shoulder blades.

Its wide flat bill of a mouth is downturned under two gaunt, yellowish eyes, one set on either side of a flattened disc of a skull.

Four tiny white claws peek out from a rounded shell at its abdomen.

Four more limbs—longer, more muscular, and reptilian—twitch at its sides.

And the whole of it rarely lingers on the ground: coiling instead around the columns as it skitter-scrambles (silently, always silently) into and out of view.

It's there for a beat, and then . . . gone.

Hiraj sits heavily on the platform ledge at the center of the commons and stares at the blackness beyond the mist.

I wait a beat, then come over and gently pat the round of his helmet.

We're fucked, Hiraj signs to me at last—and for once, his signs are surprisingly fluid. *The crazies are going to take everything.*

I know, I sign back. *I know.*

Emanuel came from the land of the crazies—his words, not ours—and on long, dull stretches of transit he would sometimes tell stories where he'd lose himself anew to the credulity of his youth. *Once, when I had only four little sols, there was a demon in my village*, he'd say—even if, during other shifts, he'd be the first to dismiss all talk of demons as nonsense.

"Except in the sack," he'd add with a wink at Case, who would roll her eyes and click her tongue at him while he was floating past.

In stories from Emanuel's childhood, the exorcists around him were always okay with modern tech right until they weren't. Sometimes they were even more enthusiastic about new upgrades than other technicians on the station—all for the greater glory of God, right? If they were mechanics, they worked on power conversion problems with great seriousness, or stress-tested the hull of a ship in dock with perfect fealty to design specs and underlying propulsion principles. If they were flight specialists, they'd rattle off ship stats without missing a beat, and calculate escape velocities for complex nav missions off the cuff.

But it's like a switch flipped whenever it came to sourcing perceived aberrations in human beings or other parts of nature. Even if they still performed all the official protocols required under such circumstances—adjusting filtration systems, recommending diagnostics tests, talking to HR—the exorcists of Buendia-4 would accept no other baseline explanation for a contaminated hydroponics crop, a baby with a birth defect, or a partnership in highly disruptive disrepair: Only "demons" would do.

No Devil in the throttle—but always in the hand upon it!

Emanuel bore arm, back, and neck tats from many of his people's formative stories, which came from wildly different traditions thrown together on evac shuttles out from different worlds. Demonology has had many gods over the centuries; and yet, when each variation of "supreme good" fades from refugee groups building new lives, only the Devil reliably remains. Who can say why for sure, but maybe it's more resilient because of its greater explanatory power, when it comes to all the things that can happen to a man out in the abyss. Did a god cause Emanuel to trip and crack his helmet open on a twist of metal on the hull? Obviously not—but then, who? The Devil stands waiting when an answer is required.

"Cosmic goodness! Ha! What an idea to try to get a spaceman to swallow," Riviera once noted, in the middle of Emanuel's tall tales of demon hunts on Buendia-4. "Easier to see all the places where things go wrong, for sure. Hard to see where many of them go right."

I remember Emanuel's slow and sly grin then. It was a beautiful thing, but also as heartbreaking as seeing a seed sprout where it wasn't supposed to.

Emanuel wasn't smiling from amusement, exactly. There was a pain in his eyes that suggested he'd learned long ago to transform grief into laughter.

"Want me to point them out to you, prima?" he'd said.

"What?"

"The good stuff, when it happens?"

Riv threw up her hands. "Boy, tell me all—a girl's got to be prepared, you know?"

"Okay, prima," Emanuel had said, softly and seriously. "I will."

And apparently, even after death, in Riviera's dreams he did.

But whenever I heard Emanuel's stories about demon hunts, I always found myself listening *through* them: picking out the deeper symbolic language in each one; learning the surrounding culture from what was and wasn't said about them.

And honestly, there was a method to the madness of the exorcists—at least on a small scale, if the exorcists were family, too. After all, if you settle on a remote asteroid, in a fragile community that needs cohesion to survive, you can't afford for some human or environmental disruption to shatter everyone's confidence in themselves, each other, or the project. So whenever exorcists leapt out of their regular lives to perform a ritual of reassurance, however ridiculous it sounded, what they were really doing was bringing people together in hard times.

Whether or not everyone on Buendia-4 believed in demons, they got a story out of the hunts, didn't they? And they could bond with other locals over that story for years to come.

Were they really "crazies", then, as Emanuel called them? Maybe, but so were we on the *Ember*, with our own little rituals to cope with life in the abyss, and with the latest absurd dictates from the strange, mad gods of Interplanetary.

(And did that make Eskin a "demon"? Oh, but that would be easier, wouldn't it? Then we could send an exorcist after him, and be cleansed of his influence for good!)

Here's what I'll suggest, then—as one old coot talking to ghosts in his head about different demon-hunters across the cosmos: There's a difference between the station-bound "crazies" of Emanuel's youth and the exorcists taking to the stars on a grand mission of galaxy-wide purgation. The latter are grifters—stage performers, power-seekers—exploiting local coping mechanisms to their own political and economic ends. They don't seem to care how many communities they upturn with their distressing displays, so long as they get paid.

And if they get to Alaru first?

There'll be no city here when they're through.

Not even the mist system will survive.

And the crystalline dead, tucked away in their tombs?

Since they can't be converted, they'll be pulverized.

To the outrage of the rest of the system? Eh, maybe. Oh, sure, the forums will have a wild ride of a news cycle, but who's going to stop the exorcists, in the end? Their way here is being paved by people who (dissatisfied by the lack of living aliens?) are content to watch the planet burn—at least, if the right story of "healing" can be attached to the brutal act.

Sometimes you really have to wonder if Interplanetary was ever a good idea.

Or leaving Old Earth.

Or crawling up onto its good green landscape in the first place.

Who knows? Maybe the shores on Old Earth were our own "mist" system; and though they tried their best for millions of years, eventually they weren't enough to keep us out.

Look now at what we've wrought.

Hiraj crouches on one of the platform steps, watching the smudge of that alien shadow flit into and out of view by the distant corridors. The first time he swears, I think it's still from shock—but when I realize he might be onto something, calculating and tempted to muse out loud about it, I tap him on the shoulder and get him to look at me. Shaking my head, I make a cutting motion with my hand at my neck.

It's not formal sign language, but the gesture should be clear enough: *Don't speak on comms. Don't leave anything on record.*

Hiraj obliges, but with a few halting signs of his own: *I HAVE AN IDEA. LANGUAGE WE SEEK.*

The last three signs are literally "language," "we," and "seek," stilted and without context. What language? Ours? The way we do damage control?

But since he's the xenobiologist, it occurs to me that he might mean the aliens. *Their* language? Has he figured something out about them from a mere flicker in the mist?

Intrigued, I gesture at our entry route.

Back to camp?

He agrees. There, we can talk outside the suits; and the way back will give us more time to reflect on other structures. But first, I try to see the city the way he's seeing it—the way that somehow clicked the moment the "ghost" became real for him, too. The burnished garnet pillars. The way this figure wraps around them, for a brief flicker—here and gone. Like a recording? Something caught in a buffer of memory? But if so, what memory? Stored where?

It's easy to forget that there are layers to everything and everyone. Emanuel doubled as a pilot and mechanic on the *Ember*, but his greatest love was reserved for solo recon missions in the solar skiff—even if they did spook him first. Hiraj, meanwhile, uses his talents so often for hydroponics that it sometimes slips my mind he's no stranger to geochem, too. Back on Clorus-5, he was our best tracker for lost cattle; now, he's great at sourcing signs of past life in mineral deposits on world-scouting missions.

Still, a "ghost-like" flicker moving between structures is hardly the same as finding ancient fossils or trace elements indicative of amino acids in the dust. So how did his skittish, colt-like mind leap so quickly from dread, to shock, to an insight that I'd missed?

As we walk back, I pull up our initial scans of the city. They carry profiles for most objects within its borders, but I still fail to register anything that explains the image in the mist. The pillars catch my notice, though, and I think through related use-cases. Metal-infused garnet shows up in solid-state laser systems: some critical for humanity's leap deeper into the stars. These pillars aren't lasers themselves, though (proper lasing rods have serious thermal strain and consistency issues at much, *much* smaller diameters, and these are massive pieces half-buried in the ground), but it occurs to me that a space-bound culture developed from related industry might have incorporated some of the tech into general aesthetic principles.

Back on Clorus-5, we were so proud of our agriculture that affectations of animal skin and related artifacts found their way even into digital wall décor. It was also local custom to tie a bit of leather loosely around the wrist of a newborn, so that they would always have "the land" with them. Hiraj's and mine had broken and been lost years ago, but sometimes I still feel the ghost of that old habit around my wrist.

Still, after rolling this possibility in my mind like a pebble on my tongue, I shake my head and chide myself: *Silly reductivist thinking.*

Case doesn't do much teaching anymore, but she used to be a sight to behold when giving new recruits and interns a walkthrough of Interplanetary procedures, back before the *Ember* started to catch more far-flung missions, and training cycles were left to captains and crews that lingered planetside with council sponsors and government officials.

If Case were in my mind just now, listening to me spout off about a whole culture based on one random tidbit about garnet pillars, I know she'd be knocking on my skull with a reminder from basic training about first encounters with different colonies:

"Don't! Extrapolate! From! Single! Data! Points!"

And that was fair. If the *Ember* crash-landed on a distant world, only to be discovered centuries later by an alien species, what ridiculous things would their forensics teams—or fanatic missionaries—say about us? Would they view the packets of vintage that Riv and Case knock back as part of a sacred ritual? Would they read our everyday belongings as other articles of cult worship? Would we be classified as exorcists, fetishists, prophets—or demons? Would they raise up our skulls to terrify their young?

The thought sends a twinge of . . . something . . . through my weary chest. Is it grief?

Sort of. An anticipatory subset, let's say: sorrow at the thought of being misunderstood by whatever world lies ahead. Even if all our corpses were found floating around the husk of the dead ship, aliens sent to study our ruins could only ever scrape the surface of who we were.

Would they have any idea of the ghost we'd been living with for many cycles?

Could their historical survey ever hope to capture how Emanuel haunts our dreams?

Back at camp, Hiraj takes off his helmet as if the mere act has taken him halfway to ecstasy. I want to make a joke about it, except that I'm still fumbling with mine—the helmet, I mean—because my hands sometimes feel as old and tired as my hearing and my sight.

Hiraj's dark hair is plastered in straggly lines and curls to his perspiring skin, but he's too caught up in his thoughts to notice. His gaze shoots out to somewhere beyond a poster of emergency decontamination protocols affixed to the storage cabinet opposite his bunk. I set my helmet beside me on mine, then idly tap on its arc of glass to get his attention.

"Well?" I say at last, when that doesn't work.

Hiraj bolts upright and shakes his head, his hands open and gesturing before him.

"You saw that, right? Tell me you saw that."

Amusement strikes me first. I took him to the city to show him, didn't I? But then I remember that my oldest mate, for all his tedious worries for me in recent cycles, is also no novice to the field. He wouldn't state the obvious. He wouldn't be *interested* in the obvious.

"You said you have an idea. What's this language you were on about?"

Hiraj shakes his head. "In the movements. You know how some insects communicate with dances? I know we keep wondering why there are no interfaces, no clear signs of language on any of the pillars—but that's thinking like a human, Rom. Xenobiology 101. This species . . . they don't wear clothes, they don't carry things with them, but that flicker in the mist . . . "

I lean back, suitably struck.

"It's not exactly moving from point A to point B."

"But you'd never get that just from the bodies in the crypt, would you? You'd need to see a real one to be sure. Those pillars . . . they might not be for show. What if they used those posts to communicate?"

I let a curl of a smile serve as reply, thinking again about my leap to lasers. Some *are* used for communication purposes, but not like he's thinking. My oldest friend is fixated more on the material object itself: the *pillar* part, not the garnet. Maybe the aliens just like the color. Maybe the garnet, infused with metallic elements, dazzles their optic systems differently. Either way, Hiraj laughs at last, passing a hand over his sweat-drenched face.

"I know, I know. Emanuel would love this. Aliens communicating by stripper pole."

"Minus the stripping."

"Unless they lost a bet just before we got here, and *that's* why they've got no clothes."

We chuckle together, then Hiraj scratches at the back of his head again. "But it's possible, right? And maybe they use pheromones, too? Only, it's been so long to notice anything else, and those sensors are so good at clearing detritus from the air."

I stand to get Hiraj a fresh sterile cloth. I'm kicking myself as I do, though, for not having considered that the alien city's intense cleanliness might serve to purify the air for language exchange. If a species relies on scent to communicate, it will surely want to clear any background "noise," no?

"Possible," I agree. "Smell and movement could work, but it's hard to imagine a species getting to the point of space travel without other forms of communication. No written records at all? Just dance? How does one communicate dance and smell at long distances?"

"We use vids just fine, don't we?"

"You think they have smell-o-vision?"

Hiraj shrugs. "Spitballing. Breaking from human assumptions. Roll with me here."

I nod, and I try to.

"You're probably right that we've missed a memory buffer somewhere. There has to be, or else how did we see that . . . "—but here I hesitate, trying not to default to dangerous terms around mention of the alien figure—"dancer in the mist?"

"It must be in the pillars themselves. Or maybe in the air? We haven't fully tested everything, and we don't have the equipment to look at the mist more carefully. We're just scouts; we'd need at least a terraforming team to check for alternative nanotech."

But of course, Interplanetary hasn't sent any of the usual science crews. It's just us and whatever nut jobs get here first. I send up another curse to Eskin, long may he choke on it.

Hiraj seems to sense my grievance. Almost in consolation, he adds: "The pillars would be easier, of course. With all the metals infused in the garnet . . . we've been assuming they're random, but maybe it's circuitry after all—just, not the type we're used to. Something more three-dimensional, using geometries we don't usually, and doing more with far less generated energy. You just gonna hold onto that forever?"

This last, he says while pointing at the cloth I'd stood to retrieve for him. I'd forgotten all about it—wringing it in my hands as we talked. I hand it to him, we make eye contact, and some of his animation fades. He knows. I know, too.

"If we only had more time," he says at last. "This is going to require a lot more study."

I sit heavily on my bunk while he dries his neck and face as best he can, scrubbing sweat-salt from his hair and skin. It feels like an especially muggy night on Alaru. The day-critters have all tagged out, and the jungle is full of different songs, even if I can only catch some of the sharper notes from each of them. I'm itchy from perspiration as well, but lack Hiraj's compulsive need to scratch. My body feels thin at its extremities: my limits to hearing and touch only growing now that I'm out of the suit.

Maybe I'm becoming more ghost-like myself. Practicing, at least. A little longer in this life, and all my atoms will spread out every which way, into the depths of the cosmos.

"You thought like a bug today, though," I say to try to cheer Hiraj. "That's not too shabby. You ever thought of going into xenobiology? It suits you."

Hiraj rolls his eyes, then sinks back on his bunk, towel tossed over a railing.

"What we *need* is to think like the crazies. If we want to protect this site, we need bug-repellant, but for fanatic pilgrims. There has to be something that'll keep them away."

I snort. "What, like a wiggle-dance to ward off invaders?"

"Exactly. A performance that would blow them out of the water."

"Stars," I correct.

"Stars," Hiraj amends.

We let the silence settle, such as it is. In the distance, something is always lowing and something is always growling, and something is always chirping in between. Just like humanity.

"The antithesis of faith isn't disbelief," he says eventually, staring at the ceiling. "Those two feed off each other. Cultists grow stronger by pitting themselves against an enemy."

"But we're not really dealing with *faith*-faith, either," I add, thinking of Emanuel's exorcists on Buendia-4. "Faith is just their cover. This is business."

"A grift," Hiraj agrees. "So what defeats a grift? And don't say exposure to the light."

I laugh. "Wasn't going to. What light, with Eskin in charge of the council?"

But Hiraj rolls onto his side, looking intently at me, his eyes bright. "What?" I say. "What?"

He shakes his head and flops back. He doesn't need to say it. I've known him forever. He was going to say that Emanuel would know the answer—and he's right. Smart kid, far better attuned to the subtle absurdities of forum life than we old stinkers ever were.

The itch returns, this time deep in my chest.

I send up a ping to the *Ember*, checking in.

Case and Riv heap a wealth of updates on us while we change and eat. We let the glow of their projections fill base-camp as they show us the state of that ridiculous space race. Fetishists, prophets, exorcists—all in the running still, as if someone with a ton of chits was purposely gaming the contest to keep things even. The competitive mood is all-consuming, too: intense enough that there are already reports of deaths from fans/followers trying all sorts of drastic promo stunts to get their chosen missions fully funded. But what's especially striking is how *serious* it all seems; how the whole initiative keeps getting elevated to the level of an existential crisis—a matter of "if not now, then when?" for its participants.

Eskin's not helping, either, with the way he speaks for council in a related news brief. He's not expressly endorsing any of the groups in this mad trek to Alaru, but the way he talks about the "gravity" of this latest Interplanetary-endorsed private mission has more militaristic overtones than any of us are used to—and yet, we recognize it for what it is.

Or at least, Riviera does, from her haunted early days on Old Earth, when her family first fled the terror of corporate forces helping to finish off tons of small settlements. Eskin, she notes, has found a way to propagate a myth of danger here, of some terrible lurking menace in need of immediate spiritual redress on Alaru, without putting himself at risk of legal consequences for whipping up a mob. His whole performance would be clever enough to merit the crew's admiration, if it weren't so depraved and chilling.

"What do we do if they show up together?" Hiraj asks. "Let them duke it out in orbit?"

"Duke it out, nuke it out, same difference." Case waves her hand on screen.

Riv laughs. "Hey now, boys, don't you go temptin' the captain here with a good time."

I want to lean into her teasing, but the situation's starting to feel too close, and too suffocating. "How far off are they?" I ask.

Riviera flicks the screen to show their route. I surprise myself with relief.

"They all have to go through the same transport dock on Marshall first. And you know they'll have to sit tight with customs there—Eskin or no Eskin on council."

Case shoots me a curious look. "You got a contact there, Rom? Planning on a little terrorism before they get through? Want some pointers, if so?"

"That settles it," says Hiraj, before whistling. "Captain's out for blood tonight."

We look at Riviera, who raises her hands. "Oh no. Don't you go blamin' this one on me! We're not knocking back vintage 28-7 up here, if that's what you think."

"I didn't say it," I say.

"But you know . . . " Riv continues, stroking her chin. She has gray hairs there that half the time don't bother her. Today, though, she's giving one of them a serious tug.

"What is it, Riv? Did Emanuel leave you a vision?" Hiraj this time.

"Always," she says softly. Then she taps her screen, though all we can see from our side is the shift of her shoulders. "But mostly, he says we're not looking at this right, which—boy, I tell him, tell us something we don't know, you know?"

Case looks at her closely. "You think we're missing something in the news briefs?"

"He guarantees we are." And Riv says this so emphatically, we know better than to disagree or tease, or to move the conversation back too fast to hard facts over dreams.

"Well, all right then," says our captain. "Let's look it over, then. Everything they're saying about Alaru, everything they're doing. What's missing? Or what's right in front of us, that we're not seeing?"

We review their claims about the aliens together—and not just because of Riv's dream, but because we want the dream to be true. We want there to be some "out" that we simply haven't noticed yet. In the prophets' press materials, we find the usual grand stories of sacrificial altars, temples dedicated to the worship of foul nether beings, and intergalactic conspiracies that involve using Alaru to tear a hole in the fabric of this reality. From images in that first report, we learn that the exorcists have repurposed the hexagonal commons to play up their cult-ritual angle, and some artists have synthed videos to illustrate how rivers of blood might flow through the alien corridors. Apparently, this river of blood is supposed to . . . activate a citywide circuit system and bring the whole compound alive?

As for the fetishists, they think the pillars are made up of remains—because the aliens in the tombs were crystallized, right? So, what if the whole city was forged from the mineralized elements of their enemies, ground into a fine powder and molded into trophies that explain the absence of any more obvious cultural artifacts?

"Points for creativity, but what is *wrong* with our species?" mutters Hiraj, after we've gone through a dozen examples of similar demon-alien lore, all buried in project announcements and press releases for the three major fanatic missions rushing toward us.

I tend to agree. We humans have a habit of projecting our fears onto the unknown. Forget awe and humility in the wake of our first concrete proof of other highly sentient beings: it's all a game to us—or maybe an extension of our inability to tell where we begin and end.

Case is the first to an answer (to her own question, not Hiraj's) because of course she is. Because she and Emanuel were always a dream team within our greater team.

"That's how we'll break them," she says with a triumphant smile. "We can't attack directly—they want us to do that."

"If we do," I agree, "we'll only be giving the impression they were right all along."

Hiraj looks at Case, then at me. "But if we don't focus on them . . . " His face pales as the solution hits him, too.

"Oh. Oh, captain, no. You're not seriously thinking we should . . . ?" But oh, oh yes, we are.

Riv and I figure it out next, and then we all look at each other with a kind of haunted resignation. We've got to make this place look ridiculous on its own merits, without mentioning or entertaining these fanatics and their own tall tales at all. The reason we keep losing—to the council, to the forums, to all of the "crazies" out there—is that we're not trained in fighting absurdity with absurdity. But if we want to keep Alaru safe from those extremists, we need to make this place look pathetic, and quickly. We need to deflate all the prestige that each mission thinks it's going to pull from getting here first.

Are actual scientists going to hate us?

Will we be pilloried in every history text written by sane people from here on out?

Mocked as the crew too stupid to know what an incredible find it had on hand?

Probably. But if we succeed, Alaru's mysterious city will still be *around* to be studied, and for someone to disprove all the mind-numbingly awful things we're about to say about it.

I sign at the ship. *Off record?*

Case starts to protest. "We're not on—!"

But Riv holds up a finger. She knows. In times like these, one can't be too careful. She ducks out of view, and we wait a bit, while she tinkers with the feed. When she returns, it's with two thumbs up. *Off record.*

I breathe out nice and slow before we begin to hash out the details. This is possibly my last sane breath for the next while—or maybe my first breath in four cycles.

Either way, it feels a lot, I realize, like finally letting go.

That night, before the four of us are set to start our little "wiggle-dance" for the good of the greater system, I dream the dream where Emanuel is talking to me, and makes no sense.

What strikes me this time, though, is that it doesn't matter. Even if I can't understand a word he's saying, or a gesture he's making, just his presence is enough.

And shouldn't it always have been?

Hiraj and I were tired hands at this space gig when he first joined our crew, and we had no idea how long he'd last among four crotchety old crewmates. Surely he'd want to be with people his own age, and not simply sucking up every luxury of youth whenever we hit port.

What could we four possibly have given him that he couldn't get better elsewhere?

Why stick it out—and die, as it so happened—for our decrepit asses?

But in my dream, at long last, even this question seems foolish. It's as if the universe is knocking on my helmet now, thudding against every haptic sensor I still have and ever owned, to say to me: *What's human language, anyway, but an elaborate way of confounding feeling?*

Emanuel stayed on because he was one of us.

And Emanuel stays on now, with us in our dreams and memories, for the same reason.

We were home to one another. Maybe not forever. Maybe only ever as a kind of *promise* of home, down the line. But still, it was a start—like a poster slapped to one of the walls of the *Ember*, reading "Coming Soon! A Place for All of You!"

So even though Emanuel can't hear me, and certainly doesn't act like he understands me in my dreaming, I tell him our plans for Alaru. I tell him that we're "accidentally" going to leak to the discovery forums that this whole place is an unfinished model city, a busted real-estate venture complete with corny ads begging people to resettle. Oh, and not an alien *state* project, either—no, no! This fuck-up was private, corporate, and abandoned in a rush. From the remaining bare-bones architecture, you can tell that whoever designed this cookie-cutter disaster seriously cut corners, so no wonder the investors fled! In fact, that's probably how this species operates in general: tons of failed business ventures littering the galaxy; junk builds left over after each start-up collapses and its primary stakeholders bolt.

And the more we talk about this economic failure of a species—Case and Riviera, me and Hiraj—the stupider the aliens will become. We'll say that the crypt isn't even a real crypt—just a lousy showroom filled with miniature representations of how the apartments were supposed to look when occupied, if these bumbling fools could ever get their funding sorted out. We'll talk about the route we took into the city as a sign that even the alien workers couldn't stand to stay in this dump while setting up fixtures for it: they needed constant breaks from this disaster of a build just to keep going as long as they did. We'll criticize every part of its structure as an utter embarrassment—the overall design, a complete and irredeemable mess.

Hiraj has even figured out how to spin a story about the "ad copy" dance he saw on the pillars, as if the alien display was close kin to some desperate billboards he'd seen once in New Oslo, to "exorcise" all rumors about ghosts. (We thought about adding a line about stripper poles to Hiraj's performance, but can't risk anything that sounds too sinful; it all has to seem boring and loser-ish, like these aliens are the last kids you'd want on your relay team.)

We won't do it all in one take, of course. We'll stagger this commentary over shifts and interactions, and we'll use some of my AugMind sketches (with a few tweaks that no one's going to be able to check through two layers of recording device—a screen through a screen!) to add to the overall authenticity for any feed-watchers who catch our "accidental" transmissions, then blast them to the forums in time for everyone to see them just as the first of the extremists' ships dock on Marshall, awaiting clearance to proceed.

Then, with any luck, all our offhand comments about how crappy this alien world is will become the stuff of spoof memes that deflate the whole project. We'll tank Eskin's investment hype cycle, and turn prominent investors and missionaries into overnight jokes.

Hey, if a few offhand words in an Interplanetary report could get us into this . . .

Well, there have been stupider turns in human history, have there not?

Anyway, I tell Emanuel all of this and more, and it makes no impression—he's still going through the motions in my dreams: a flicker in the mist, an echo in my memories—and yet, somehow that's more comforting than if he'd given me the sympathy I've been aching to hear all along: from him, from you, from whatever other ghosts are still out in the abyss. Let language and reason break down, if they must. Let us see ourselves for what we truly are, as fragile little primates not long for life itself—and reacting, always reacting, more on a hunch or a feeling than out of any clear, steady vision for the world we want to come.

But so what?

If we're still here to keep dreaming—if that breakdown in reason *permits* us to still be here to keep dreaming, against all cosmic flukes and bad odds—then maybe that's enough.

When I wake on the first morning of Operation: Mediocrity, I don't move all at once. I stare at the ceiling until dawn comes and Hiraj stirs, and then I pretend that I've just woken as well; and we look at each other, bleary-eyed, as if we're back on Clorus-5. As if doing what we're about to do is just another chore on the ranch, like bringing in the cattle before a storm.

Outside camp, Alaru's morning songs seem to be in good form, and the rain's left a glossy finish on everything around us. The whole jungle seems to creak and moan as we do: just another set of old, pungent creatures shambling out from bed and our memories.

I think I'll crack the seal on my helmet, after we've finished our first call to the *Ember*.

It'll be harder for me to hear the world without my comms, or my haptics—but it might be nice to breathe a more honest stench again, after all is said and done.

ABOUT THE AUTHOR

M. L. Clark is a writer, editor, and translator originally from Canada, now based in Medellín, Colombia. Clark's science fiction appears in a range of venues including *Analog, Clarkesworld, F&SF,* and *Lightspeed.* Book and other media reviews appear in *Strange Horizons,* while genre advocacy through SFWA's Pubs Crew occupies a big role in a life otherwise spent where the wild things are.

The Hanging Tower of Babel
WANG ZHENZHEN, TRANSLATED BY CARMEN YILING YAN

"Hey there—comrade—are you also part of the—Space Industry—Development Program—First Cohort? I'm Zhang Haoyu—second lieutenant—pleased to meet you." The man in front of me spoke in choppy fragments. He extended his hand, heedless of the puzzled looks coming from all around us.

"Hello, Comrade Zhang Haoyu, I'm your superior, here to relay an order from Command—you are to remain on Earth for now, and await liftoff at a later date." My scalp was itching from the looks the bystanders were giving us, but I kept my posture strained ramrod-straight as I imitated an army man's booming way of speaking. I projected my latest résumé beside me, pretending it was my military credentials.

"Yes, sir!" He clicked his heels, a forceful movement that made only a faint muffled sound, and lifted a hand to me in salute. Salute complete, he even thought to straighten his uniform cap, though his fingers touched only the soft contours of a knit hat. The incorrect detail sent a faint crease of puzzlement down his face, but it faded immediately. His lips pressed once more into the professional firmness of a military man.

"Comrade, our commanding officer has already briefed me on your place of residence. He's appointed me to escort you home. I'd like to ask you to refrain from leaving your residence in the absence of further orders."

"I'm grateful for my superiors' consideration." He bowed slightly and followed me out of the terminal, toward the parking lot.

As we approached the car, he caught my sleeve. "Son, I forgot you again, didn't I?"

I angled my head faintly, avoiding his gaze, saying nothing. This time, he'd caught on. But what about the next time?

"It's raining. Don't catch a chill, come on."

My father Zhang Haoyu was a hero. At the end of the previous century, when the completion of the "Stairway to Heaven" in Indonesia had sounded the clarion of humanity's mass-scale entry into space, my father had out-competed a hundred and twenty of his elite peers for a place among the first cohort to ascend the Stairway, the leading edge of the space development wave. Before departure, he'd even represented the entire Development Corps in an interview with the media, where he'd casually tossed out the term, "Industrial Workers of the Cosmos," that became the label and self-identity for his cohort. For thirty years, he'd fulfilled his mission and duty to the utmost, achieving countless great deeds, and receiving too many awards to fit on his chest.

But behind every hero were others paying a quiet price. Out of every year, he spent ten months in space on average. You normally remember someone by their presence, but in my memory, he existed largely as his absence. He wasn't there when Grandma passed away. He never showed his face at a single parent-teacher conference, and birthdays and the like were too much to ask. At my mother's funeral, every one of his in-laws gave him the cold shoulder. Aside from the massive sums wired like clockwork into Mom's bank account, he was AWOL for practically my entire childhood.

No, it's a bit of an exaggeration to say my entire childhood. Even now, I still remember my first impression of his face: a very high-resolution face, though a little laggy, framed by the screen of Mom's cell phone. I would dream a lot at that age. In those dreams, the solar arrays reflected a glowing haze across those 6.5 inches of outer space, and through the haze, a multitude of men in red-and-white uniforms would turn in unison to look at me with kindly eyes, waiting for me to call them "Papa."

And there's one other thing that could count as presence in my childhood memories: a metal box, very finely made, but totally without identifying features, so that you couldn't even tell which side of it was the front. On the eve of one of his departures from Earth, my father had sat at my bedside and set the box on the nightstand. I lay on the bed, very sleepy, with only a vague impression of his blurry silhouette. He said that if one day, a strange man suddenly came to the house, I should give the box to the man. He'd know how to open it.

That little box became one of my childhood toys; I was too young then to realize what the box must've contained. When I was a little older, and had entered the primary school for the children of space workers, I discovered that seemingly all of my classmates also had a little box at home. After school, we'd get together and try all sorts of tricks to open them, but we never did succeed. One day in second grade, a strange man suddenly appeared in class to call away one of the girls. She never returned. Later, we heard that she'd transferred to another school. We didn't know what it had to do with the boxes, but even so, everyone stopped bringing them up, and soon we forgot about them.

The conversations through the phone screen, the farewell at my bedside . . . I still remembered all of it clearly, but he'd forgotten entirely.

"We've confirmed it's Alzheimer's disease. Which variant is unclear, but we can be certain that it's progressed to the middle stages. Frankly, given the length of time Comrade Zhang Haoyu spent in space, he's doing very well."

The doctor didn't beat around the bush. Both my father and I nodded calmly. Out of the Industrial Workers of the Cosmos who'd once lived and worked alongside my father, the vast majority were now either buried or basically vegetative. Next to them, his present condition ought to be reason to celebrate.

In fact, aside from the very low rates of economic return, Alzheimer's was also a major reason behind the abrupt end to space development. Twenty years ago, many of the retired members of the Development Corps had started experiencing symptoms of memory loss and dementia. They were getting diagnosed with neurodegenerative diseases at many times above the normal rate, and when tested, it was found that the damage was almost entirely concentrated in a few specific areas of the brain. In the end, more than half the former corps were determined to have developed Alzheimer's.

The research that followed indicated that this may well have been the result of long-term exposure to high doses of deep space radiation, a consequence that couldn't have been detected in those early years of space industry. When you were working in space, it was impossible to avoid all kinds of radiation exposure, no matter how good your protective measures. Most illnesses resulting from the radiation could be treated with drugs and radiation therapy, but confronted with man's still-uncharted hippocampus and dentate gyrus, modern medicine remained helpless. As a result, many of those once bold and spirited heroes became tongue-tied elderly children who couldn't talk without needing someone to wipe their drool.

"Then, how long will I still maintain my cognitive abilities?" my father asked directly, as if inquiring as to the service life of a machine.

"It's hard to say. Anywhere from a few weeks up to a few years. And your cognitive abilities won't just decline linearly. Sometimes you'll find yourself re-recalling something, regaining some abilities, only to lose them again. I've seen a late-stage patient calculating differential equations with pen and paper, but that's no guarantee of anything."

"Okay. So what can I do to slow down this process?"

"Regularly engaging in moderate mental exercise, like reading and writing. A fixed daily routine. And most importantly, your son's solicitude."

"No, I think I can—"

The doctor cut him off. "I know what you want to say. All you space workers are the same, insisting you can take care of yourselves. If you try, it inevitably ends in either forgetting to take your pills, or taking them several times a day. Trust me, Alzheimer's disease needs to be confronted with you and your family as a team. There's no shame in it."

We left the hospital together. My father told me to leave him be as much as possible. He could take care of himself. I said okay.

After that day, he seemed to return to some of his habits from military life.

Every morning, his alarm would wake me from the other room. He'd get up at 7:30, fold his blanket into a neat "tofu block," take a morning jog, then breakfast on a bowl of porridge with pickled vegetables and an egg. He shaved off the graying hair at his temples, and bought an eyebrow razor, trimming his unruly tufts into order. He'd sit at the windowsill and read books, mostly difficult textbooks on subjects related to space development—he'd in fact contributed to and edited some of them. A couple decades ago, these were the majors that all the college students were flocking to. I'd tangled with these texts myself during my college years, only to find that, not only were they beyond my understanding, they also wouldn't help me with finding work. Purely looking at habits and quality of life, I thought that he seemed terrifically healthy, and that I was the one who was sick.

But the changes came in the end.

Peng!

The china cup fell, shards scattering across the floor. Coffee ran along the cracks between the floorboards. My father stared at the mess on the floor in bafflement, as if trying to comprehend the existence of gravity. Suddenly he realized: this was Earth, not space. Surprised, I started to rise to clean it up, but he lifted a hand to stop me. He made the mess, so he should do the cleaning. He considered it a matter of personal dignity.

Peng!

A wave of flames boiled up, scorching black marks across the white wall of the kitchen. I hurriedly grabbed the fire extinguisher and blasted away wildly. When the flames died and I broke apart the milk-white hardened foam, I found black charcoal, the original food ingredients long since rendered unrecognizable. This time, I really didn't see why I should stand aside and watch as he mopped and scrubbed. We cleaned the kitchen together, and then I helped him order takeout.

Peng!

I jolted violently awake in my bed, my back covered in cold sweat. The house was very quiet, but an enormous noise still seemed to echo in my brain. Good, it had been only a nightmare.

I quietly snuck into my father's bedroom. The sound of his snores remained steady. I opened his drawer: amid the neatly arranged notebooks lay an old-fashioned, real-deal handgun. The right side clearly had an ejector port for casings. I wasn't a gun aficionado myself, but I remembered what my father had once mentioned to me when I was very small: in order not to create space debris, they'd been issued sidearms that only shot caseless ammunition. I groped around a little, surreptitiously took out all the bullets, and returned the gun to its place.

"I asked the doctor yesterday. He said it's fine to have a few sips a day." I sat across from my father and poured him a small cup. I'd rarely seen him drink, but I'd read books—in the stories, whether your father was a farmer, laborer, or CEO, a dad-son heart-to-heart never took place without a glass.

"We never drank in space. If there's something you want to say, say it." He spread the book pages-down over his thigh, propped forearms on knees, and looked at me.

"It's nothing. I just wanted to hear your stories about space," I ventured, taking a sip myself.

"You can watch the documentaries. I said quite a bit in those." His voice was calm.

"I want to hear something I haven't heard. It'll be a nice exercise for you, too," I laughed.

He shut the book and sat silently, looking down, thinking. It was some time before he spoke.

"I . . . had a brother-in-arms, Old Yu. Very tall guy, combed his hair in this big swept-back hairdo. At the time, he was my assistant. We'd do tethered hull crawls together." He was remembering these details with effort.

"Oh, yeah, I remember him. He came to our house when I was little. I even rode on his back."

"Ah . . . did he?" I'd interrupted his train of thought. The narrative came to an abrupt halt as he turned to trying to recall the details I'd mentioned.

"Yeah, on my fifth birthday. Uncle Yu and Uncle Cheng came down together."

"Oh, yes, right. I remembered once you mentioned Old Cheng. Yes, they came by." He nodded.

I knew he was pretending. The year of my fifth birthday, only Old Yu had come.

"Anyway, what happened to Uncle Yu?"

"He died."

"He died?"

"One time on the outside, his RCS—his thruster system, for adjusting motion—started malfunctioning. One set of nozzles went out of control and he couldn't turn it off. He started to spin, got caught by gravity. Started to fall, bit by bit. We weren't able to save him in time. In the end, he took off his own helmet."

" . . . "

"I'm not trying to imply anything. I just think that, compared to those guys, I've ended up pretty well all things considered." My father took a sip too, to ease the atmosphere.

"Did you ever regret it all?"

"Never."

"I don't believe it."

"Why?"

"A couple days ago, when I was cleaning, I saw your drawer."

My father paused, as if struggling to make sense of what I was saying. And then he startled, like a child caught making trouble. "You went through my things?"

"I'm the primary caregiver. The doctor gave me that right. Or, to put it in your terms, it's called barracks standards." I'd prepared my self-justification long ahead of time.

He sat back down, and was silent for a long while. He finally said, "I've really never regretted it."

"Even the way you are now? You got a gun for yourself, and you nearly forgot about it."

"Yes, even so. I'd prepared myself before I ever left." Oddly, my father had calmed down. "The memory of an individual might be a puny thing, but there will always be people to remember us."

"And what will they remember? After experiencing the failure of space development, what do you expect them to remember? They'll only think of space development as the product of stupid arrogance. Your bunch wasted the futures of generations of people on that giant useless Stairway to Heaven, and in the end it was nothing more than pulling on your own hair to lift your feet off the ground!"

"Ridiculous! History will properly remember us!"

"History . . . there might well not be any more history. At least, people don't think there will be." I projected a book in front of me: *On the End of History and the Last Man*, the current bestseller. I swept my gaze over the foreword—the author had taken inspiration from the theory of a scholar from a hundred years in the past. In the scholar's era, the theory had been dismissed as a joke, but in this book, he was revered as a great prophet.

"Don't spend all day filling your head with those nonsense takes." He'd raised his voice.

"I'm not the one with dem—cognitive impairment! It's none of your business!" I raised my voice too.

"I, I—" He tried to retort, but suddenly got stuck, like a jammed cartridge. He struggled for a while, then gave up, swept up the glass, drained it in one, and slammed it back onto the table. Our heart-to-heart thus ended unhappily.

Once I calmed down, I wondered about the whole thing. Why had I fought with him? What was so important as to be worth this kind of fight? So I went back to him to talk it over, only to find him bewildered. He didn't remember any argument at all.

After that, I again had him tell stories of the past. A small portion was utterly shocking, stories of his comrades who'd died in the line of duty. Brained by debris, struck by tethers . . . there were a thousand exotic ways to die in outer space, too horrible for any news media to air. The only consolation was that the victims generally wouldn't have time for suffering and regret.

The rest of the stories were much more along the traditional lines. He told me how he'd salvaged an accident that might well have otherwise ended up in the history books, how he'd disassembled a bomb planted on the interior of the Stairway; he told me how he'd snuck rare free moments to gaze at Earth in outer space and look for his homeland, how he'd never tired of seeing the dazzling grandeur of the Milky Way. I could only relate to a small portion of what he talked about, but I had to admit, even if he really had gotten eaten by a space monster, he'd at least have lived a full and meaningful life.

But, for me, those days had barely gotten started, when a call from an unfamiliar number cut them short.

The caller claimed he was from the "Stairway to Heaven Management Committee." He told me, the great Stairway was about to be dismantled, and the Committee could provide me with a job on the project. I cussed him out as a scammer. He said it was okay, I could think on it, he would welcome me to call back when I was ready.

The next morning, my father and I saw the press conference for the "Stairway Dismantlement Plan" on TV.

In any discussion of merit, half the credit for the prosperity of my father's era of space development deserved to go to the Stairway to Heaven. Nowadays, living in the long economic depression, people could no longer even imagine how their elders had organized such monumental levels of manpower and resources to build this miracle of engineering. The Stairway to Heaven had cut the cost of a heaven-earth round-trip by 95%, and the cost of an Earth-Moon round-trip by 80%, making it possible for ordinary people to go to space. At the time, people had lavished it unstintingly with praise: it was like a dragon soaring into the nine heavens, a rainbow piercing the mists. They'd built the Tower of Babel, a miraculous conduit to the promised land.

But then the economic winter had come, and space development had come to a screeching halt. The volumes being transported on the Stairway to Heaven rapidly shrank, and within two years was down to just one percent of what they'd been at the peak, while the cost of maintenance remained constant.

And thus it became an unimaginable negative equity. Ten years ago, the income it received from shipping actually fell below the income from tourism, making it the world's most money-burning scenic site. Despite many rounds of restructuring, there was simply no way to curtail the cost of maintaining the Stairway. One company had tried cutting the drone fleet used to monitor stress changes within the Stairway by one third, and had directly caused a Level 2 accident. Worse, demolishing the Stairway with oriented blasting would also be an enormous expenditure, and none of the conglomerates wanted to foot the bill. So the whole mess dragged on. The only certainty was that human society would collapse from this colossal money-eating dragon before the next outer space boom rolled around.

By now, the problem had gotten to the point where it couldn't be put off any longer. The world's great conglomerates had come together as they rarely did, assembling a committee, which had suggested the simplest method of disassembly: only demolishing the portion below the stratosphere.

To a layman, the Stairway to Heaven resembled a tall tower, rising from the Earth with its tip in outer space. But from an engineer's perspective, it more resembled a rope dangling down from geostationary orbit. Above Indonesia, thirty-six kilometers in the sky, was the Stairway's midway relay station, from which one end of the Stairway extended toward Earth, and the other deeper into space.

In fact, the majority of the Stairway's maintenance cost came from the Earthside portion, in the troposphere region below twenty kilometers. This section was designed to endure ocean mist, typhoons, and even shock waves from mid- to close-range nuclear explosions. Meanwhile, the main expense of dismantling the Stairway came from the stretch above ten kilometers, because any space debris generated there would disperse unpredictably, without being incinerated by the atmosphere, potentially creating a disaster.

Therefore, the conglomerate committee proposed to dismantle just the twenty kilometers at either end of the Stairway to Heaven, turning it into a "geostationary orbit satellite." After that, the only expense would be the use of Hall-effect thrusters to maintain its orbital equilibrium. This would wipe out over 95% of maintenance costs at one stroke, without any unpredictable consequences. It was a thoroughly practical proposal.

Even afflicted with Alzheimer's, my father grasped the proposal more quickly than I did. He was thunderous, flicking off the TV on the spot, hurling the remote control to the floor, before sitting there to stew. I didn't tell him that someone had wanted to use the opportunity to give me a job. Making him even angrier wouldn't be good for his condition.

After some hesitation, I called that number back after all, and quietly heard out the other party's request.

To put it in simple terms, they wanted me to be a mascot, or, one of the "forgotten minority behind the grand era of space development." All I had to do was give one little speech at the opening ceremony for the Stairway to Heaven Dismantlement Project—relate a sob story about how the Space Development Plan had stolen my father from my childhood years; then bemoan the hardship of taking care of a senile old man; express some second-, third-, fourth-, and fifth-hand bargain-bin critiques of the whole business; and, finally, exhort everyone to return their gazes to Earth. It would be that simple, to give them the bit of legitimacy they needed to dismantle the Stairway to Heaven. A three-minute pledge of allegiance, and I'd earn the equivalent of three years of my salary, just like that.

The stars were lofty, and money lowly. But the trend of the times swept us all up in its current. Economic conditions were getting worse by the day. It was too exorbitant a luxury these days to gaze up at the stars.

In the end, I agreed, behind my father's back.

After the press conference about the Stairway dismantlement, my father's mood grew very low. He read fewer and fewer books. His physical condition rapidly worsened. I still had him tell me stories every day, but he was telling less by the day, and would sometimes repeat stories he'd already told.

After some days, the people, dates, and cause-and-effect in the stories began to unravel as well; he rearranged and recombined them into many different versions. Every time he told the story, he'd leave some details out, and fill in new details. I felt like I was watching the dazzling Milky Way slowly distort into Van Gogh's *The Starry Night*, then into a mere mass of colors, and finally into the undifferentiated gray-brown of the water used to rinse an artist's brushes. By the end, he would repeat a sentence over and over, or get stuck on an adjective for ages, without realizing it was happening at all. When he finally did notice, he'd grow very agitated, thumping his fists furiously on his thighs, or the table, muttering obscenities, until, moments later, he forgot the failure.

But no matter how hard he tried, he could no longer tell a complete story.

And then one day, I went out for a stroll with him, and, without any warning, he made a turn right out of my line of sight. When I realized he'd disappeared, he'd been gone for nearly five minutes. I turned on navigation, looking for him via GPS, but only found his bracelet discarded on the side of the road. The neon lights from the upper strata cast down eye-dazzling halation. The passing cars roared deafeningly. I was starting to panic. I hurriedly contacted his primary physician.

"Don't worry, this kind of thing is common in the late stage. Eight or nine out of ten he's gone to the nearest Stairway to Heaven station. You should be able to find him there."

I knew that the doctor didn't mean the about-to-be-demolished "Stairway to Heaven."

In my father's day, the Stairway to Heaven was the "Space Elevator." And these days, by "Stairway to Heaven," people meant the completely different and increasingly obsolete vertical rail system. Built with the excess production capacity from the Space Elevator, they'd once supported the functioning of these crowded hive-cities. Most of them were only a few hundred meters tall, using some of the Stairway to Heaven's technology to connect the surface with the financial centers and wealthy neighborhoods of the upper strata. If the vertical rails were becoming obsolete, it wasn't because of any advances in technology, but because of the growing gulf between rich and poor. People had gradually lost the need to travel between the upper and lower strata of a hive-city.

Aside from commonalities in design, they had almost nothing in common with the original. To dignify them with the name "Stairway to Heaven" was like calling an ant a tree. But it was these, that had pulled the vast sky forty kilometers above to the paltry distance of a few hundred meters.

I reached the Stairway terminal, and saw my father, sitting erectly, staring intently at the white words on the big red screen, as if looking for his train, or as if waiting for the comrades-in-arms meant to ride out with him. He exuded a tranquil indifference I hadn't seen in a long time, and in my strained, anxious state, it lit a new unnamable fire in my heart.

Seeing me appear in a lather in front of him, he seemed strangely surprised.

"Dad! What happened? Why did you take off the bracelet?"

My questioning brought him back to the real world. His tranquil mood quickly grew agitated again. He looked down, silent. After some time, he said, "I don't want to be forgotten."

Similar incidents happened several more times after that. I learned a script from the doctor, to pretend I was his commander, in order to cajole and trick him home.

"We can be fairly certain that it's reached the late stage. It's gone somewhat faster than I expected, but that's not your fault. Some things can't be held back."

Despite the doctor's words, I still felt a certain guilt. My father sat next to me, stiff-faced. I couldn't tell what he was thinking.

"Then, going to the Stairway to Heaven is . . . "

"Many retired corps members experience similar symptoms once their disease progresses to this late stage. It's understandable, really. That day was the highlight of their lives. Of course they'd remember it unshakably. They'll instinctively look for the tallest structure they can find and make a beeline for it. In that empty ocean of lost memories, this often becomes their final life preserver."

My father's expression was as serene as the waters of an ancient well.

"Is there anything I can do now?"

"I'm afraid there's nothing left in terms of emotional solicitude. All that's left is physical caretaking, changing diapers and so on. To tell the truth, at this stage, provided your finances allow for it, I would personally suggest that you take your father to a senior home, where the staff can provide him with more professional care. The heavy burden of caretaking without any return can be hard on a person."

"I've considered it, but I don't know if he'd want to . . . "

"By this point, it's hard for him to feel much of anything about it. Rest easy, son, you've done very well."

My father turned to me, as if wanting to say something.

"Oh, one more thing. I notice that, every time I find him at the Stairway terminal, he seems very calm, even happy. Should I regularly take him to the Stairway terminal to walk around?"

"If it makes you feel better, I don't see why not. But I fear your father won't feel anything special," the doctor said, with a little wave.

"Okay. I'll do that."

"Oh, that reminds me." The doctor dug up a rather aged-looking brochure for me. "I recommend this care center specializing in Alzheimer's disease patients. It's in a remodeled abandoned Stairway terminal, and exclusively takes in old spacefarers. It's been open for a while. The prices are reasonable, and the reviews are pretty good. You might consider sending him there."

"Thanks, but I want to do as much as I can myself."

The consultation soon ended. Just as we were about to leave the office, my father finally remembered what he'd wanted to say.

"Hello, uncle. Who are you?" He took my hand; through it, I felt a faint trembling.

In the end, I admitted, the doctor was right.

Afterward, in one of my father's more lucid periods, I had another talk with him. He, using a military tone of voice, ordered me to take him to the care center. Unable to withstand the dual assault of gentle persuasion and hard demand, I agreed. He went, "Yay," like a child.

My father sat in the wheelchair while I pushed him up the hill, gazing at the Stairway to Heaven not far away—the real Stairway to Heaven. The conglomerates had wanted me to come over and walk around the place, familiarize myself with the course of the ceremony. I'd taken the opportunity to bring my father along, hoping to use one of his lucid spells to let him see the Stairway to Heaven up close one last time.

The elements, over the years, had left many scars on the Stairway to Heaven. Even through the filter of the golden setting sun, large quantities of rusted non-structural components still poked through the curtain of nostalgia, jabbing sharply at onlookers' eyes. The non-critical sound-dampening structures had long since fallen away; the air now collided with the Stairway's protrusions, stirring into some kind of current high above, generating unsettling, arrhythmic clashing noises like a death rattle.

Very soon, the portion we saw in front of us would be obliterated in a series of meticulously designed explosions. My father was still staring dumbly as I lifted my head, estimating the distances. After the demolition, it would be hard to perceive the Stairway's presence from up close. Instead, on a clear day, people should be able to see it on the horizon. It ought to be even more striking at night, a long thin black thread cutting across the Milky Way, clearly etching out its chilly contours against the black swan down night.

I couldn't help but think of the famous story of the Tower of Babel—people coming together to build a high tower, just so they could be closer to their god. We built the Tower of Babel, but found that the gods weren't in fact there. So now we were going to take it apart.

I imagined the Stairway to Heaven after the demolition, floating in the sky—like a hanging Tower of Babel, dangling down from an infinitely high and infinitely far place, piercing the boundary between heaven and earth, but unable, despite all its might, to touch the realm of humanity.

I looked down. My father was still staring. I wanted to leave, but he tugged on my sleeve. So I draped my jacket over his shoulders and sat down, cross-legged, quietly keeping him company.

Gradually, the distant sky revealed a star or two. I didn't know their names. If my father were lucid, he could probably recognize them at a glance. He held my hand, occasionally making some meaningless mumble. I straightened so that I could see his face. In the dimness of twilight, the sockets of his eyes appeared deeply sunken, but his eyes were clear.

At that moment, I dimly felt as if I were looking at a child, looking at my father in his childhood. The doctor had said that my father's mental capabilities were currently equivalent to those of a child of five or six. Then, what was he thinking about now? Did he see in the sky his decades as an Industrial Worker of the Cosmos? That weighty history? Or was he back in childhood, quietly dreaming that one day, once he was all grown up, he'd ascend the Stairway to Heaven and soar into space?

He made some more noises, as if trying to convey something, but in the end, no sentence emerged. Yet, on that lonely hill, the wind seemed to sweep up those sounds and carry them across time, bringing with them an endless wealth of meaning. When our ancestors first lifted their heads to gaze at the stars, had they made sounds like these?

When my thoughts returned from the celestial vastness, back to reality, my father's murmurs had come to an end as well. He was hunched slightly forward, propped up on his forearms, as if thinking deeply.

In the twilight at the foot of the Stairway to Heaven, this worker of the cosmos had stopped breathing.

A small, finely-made metal box lay in front of me.

I'd found it amid my father's belongings. He must have secretly hidden it away in one of his lucid spells. I hadn't seen it since second grade in elementary school, but I knew for certain that it was the box from my memories. As a child, I hadn't known what lay inside, but now, I was ready.

I swiped with my father's retirement card, then gently pried. The box parted in response. Inside were sheets upon sheets of paper, and a black-and-white photo. The paper bore his last will and testaments, one every two years from his first ascent into space until retirement, the handwriting neat, the cadence of the sentences well-crafted.

The first will had been written before he went into space. It contained only a line of Mao's poetry:

Everywhere on the green mountains are buried the bones of the faithful/ No need to wrap the body in horsehide and bear it back.

He was really something.

The second will—two years after he went into space—bore his own words.

. . . You might not have much of an impression of Papa, but remember that Papa loves you . . . the second will was about a hundred characters. At the time, I'd just learned to speak.

. . . You memorized your multiplication tables very quickly. You deserve praise for it. I can see that you have a talent for math and the sciences. You shouldn't waste it. Study hard, and when you've grown up, you can come to space to work in Papa's place . . . This was the third will, three hundred characters. I was still in kindergarten.

. . . Take good care of Mom. She gave up a lot for our family. Now that I've gone and stubbornly died, the responsibility of the man of the house lies on your shoulders . . . This was the fourth, five hundred characters. I'd started elementary school.

. . . Yesterday, I went to see Old Yu's family. I was really gutless, I couldn't string together a single sentence. In the end, all I could do was hug the others and cry. I couldn't sleep all night. I feel like whatever I write is bloodless . . . This was the seventh. He was guilt-ridden, spending almost the whole letter talking about Old Yu's death.

. . . Don't blame Mom. She did the right thing. It's all my fault that things ended up this way. Stay with her and live well. When you're grown, do what you want to do . . . This was the tenth. That year I was twenty, and Mom had chosen divorce.

. . . Old Cheng's started having trouble with talking too. To be honest, if you see this, I'll be pretty happy. A clean death. I won't give you all trouble like Old Cheng . . . This was the fourteenth, from his last year on duty.

I finished reading all of them, and gasped down deep breaths, forcing myself not to cry.

He'd liked to say that each generation had its own destiny. I hadn't believed him at first. I'd thought the destiny of my generation was to witness the end of history. But in this moment, the understanding and empathy I'd gained, accompanying my father to see the Stairway in Indonesia, seemed to have transformed into some emotion harder to put into words. I ought to do something for them. Posterity ought to remember them.

I dialed the Committee's phone number.

Three months later.

" . . . The Committee expresses that, after the dismantlement of the Stairway to Heaven, the remaining portion will house a new 'Museum of the History of Space Development,' a semi-permanent repository for artifacts related to deceased space workers, including their wills, space suits, equipment, and so on. It's said that the original proponent of the project was the son of a space worker. He hopes that everyone can . . . "

I let out a breath. They'd listened to my suggestion. After all, from their perspective, without much outlay on their part, they could profit off of sympathy for the elders of space development, and gild themselves with an additional layer of legitimacy. It was a win-win.

A chilly north wind blew. Drops of autumn rain fell past the beehive-shaped sky-dome that separated the city strata, landing on the hologram fountain at the city center, raising half-real half-illusory ripples. I stood under the eaves, gazing at the newsreel rolling past above my head. I stood there for a long time.

When I turned to leave, I saw a child tugging on her mother, asking, what was the Stairway to Heaven. I let out a puff of white vapor, lifting my head to look at the heavens. The starry night was luminous, like my father's clear gaze.

Originally published in the
Chinese edition of *Galaxy's Edge Magazine*, Issue #15.

Translated and published in partnership with Storycom.

ABOUT THE AUTHOR

Wang Zhenzhen, a sci-fi writer and a games writer, is known for telling realistic stories in a humorous style. His stories "Minesweeper" and "Whose Funeral," published in *Science Fiction World,* were respectively selected as The Sci-Fi Stories of the Year for 2018 & 2019. He won the Fifth Morning Star Awards for Best Short Story for "The Orbiting Guan Erye," and won the Second Dook Book Awards for Best Short Story for "The Hanging Tower of Babel."

Born in China and raised in the United States, **Carmen Yiling Yan** was first driven to translation in high school by the pain of reading really good stories and being unable to share them. Since then, her translations of Chinese science fiction have been published in *Clarkesworld, Lightspeed,* and *Galaxy's Edge,* as well as numerous anthologies. She graduated from UCLA with a degree in Computer Science, but writes more fiction than code these days. She currently lives in the Midwest.

Numismatic Archetypes in the Year of Five Regents

LOUIS INGLIS HALL

Fig. 1. Gold coin, 356 P.F. (post-foundation).
Obverse: profile of Auréle, right-facing.
Legend: REGENT ETERNAL.
Reverse: Tree, fruiting (symbolizing prosperity).

This five-sorel piece is in fine condition. The design is sophisticated, improving upon the bronze Auréles minted throughout the 340s. Trees were a common peacetime motif and recur in coinage from Auréle's accession in 339 onwards.

They cut off Auréle's head and they put it on a pike above the city's third best bridge. To me, that seemed a shame. I had only just got his nose right.

It had a crook in it, Auréle's nose. A sporting accident, from his days at the Academy. He'd been playing in some intramural league, the sort of game that teenagers play with balls and sticks and plastic shields jammed across their gums. Whether it was a ball or a stick I don't know, but it left him with this pad of flesh, a thickening over the bridge, like a sticking-plaster.

In my head it was doughy, malleable. In my head I pressed down with my thumbs and watched it spread, watched the fat disperse into the caverns of his cheeks.

There had been consequences, of course. Auréle was tutored within the bounds of the Regency, afterwards. A tiny secession, an admission that the rulers of this city were a thing apart. Not even the finest schools could hold them.

That, and they executed the boy that did it.

I look back on my first portraits of Auréle with some embarrassment. Coinage is a limited medium. Detail is a rare flourish, and cameos can tend towards caricature.

I was called to the Chancellery, after our first minting. They sat me in a cool gray room and fed me sugar biscuits and told me I had made the regent into a vulture. Politely, they asked that the coins be melted down. "It doesn't work like that," I said. Money travels. Coins circulate.

The regent's face, in the hands of the people. Just watch it spread.

My canvas is inverse, miniaturized. A circular stamp held fast in a rectangular frame. I dig down into it with needle-blades. Each stroke will be raised like scar tissue on the finished artifact.

Elsewhere in the workshop, Maya strikes discs from cold metal. A greater city-state would call this place a mint, but Phuzein is not great. Her coins are born from the three of us: Maya, myself, and Quintil, whose function is to provide us with takeaway coffees from the shop across the street.

A greater city-state might have factories, it might have machines, spindle-fingered things that pass day and night in etching and engraving and packaging in neat commemorative boxes.

Maya has a hammer. We need nothing else to imprint my design, to raise a weal in soft and pregnant bronze.

Soldiers come on Wednesdays, and take our children away by the truckload.

When it happened, we downed tools. There were processions outside, or maybe riots. Voices, and the smashing of pottery. We flowed into a passing crowd, allowed it to carry us in its slow, drunken orbits.

The evening was deep into a purple dark by the time we reached the bridge. It jutted out, in silhouette. Auréle's profile, in warp and decay.

There wasn't much nose left. People had been throwing stones.

We didn't question why he died. We watched him for a while, until his dead eyes were lost behind the gloom, and then we went away.

Already, graffiti grew in red blooms across the city walls. Already, factions formed in the hum and chatter of a thronging crowd. Violence overspilled, puddled itself in street-gutters.

"What happens now?" asked Quintil, as we passed through a haze of lamp-glow. Beyond it, half-obscured, propped like sandbags against a low wall, we saw the first of the bodies.

We said nothing, and hurried across a plaza that would soon become a battlefield.

Fig. 2. Silver coin, 356 P.F. (post-foundation).
Obverse: profile of Florian, left-facing.
Legend: PHUZEIN ENDURES.
Reverse: The walled city-state of Phuzein.

This single sorel is in good condition. The portrait is basic, and Florian's depiction is consistent with Lorgado's "The Retaking of the City," composed in the same year. This painting is now held in Sub-Archive 7-Kappa-7 of the Parliament of Books, Stack P-19. The image of Phuzein, intact and triumphant, stands in contrast to the devastation and riot that brought Florian to the Regency.

Three weeks we waited, while the west of the city burned. We huddled together in the cool of the workshop, and filtered out the sounds of munitions in the distance. The metal lay stacked in quiet sheets and we did nothing to transmute it.

On Wednesdays, the soldiers failed to come. We played flick-games, sent bronze Auréles skimming into ceramic coffee cups. Maya did the best of all of us. We held a coronation, named her flick-regent. She gave a speech, and promised to be a just ruler.

I worked on my reverses. A spray of feathers, a crown, a chariot. Regents always want the same designs. I worked up a new one, an army, carefully genericized. Quintil begged and I did him one, a coffee cup, complete with waving, cartoon heat lines. It made him laugh, made the corners of his mouth tuck up into his cheeks. I told myself I hadn't noticed that.

The soldiers came, and it wasn't a Wednesday at all, and told us Phuzein had a regent once more. His name was Florian, and he was here to make the city whole again. Maya asked how much of the city Florian had kicked down in the first place, and the soldiers took out their wooden batons and smashed apart a wall of shelves.

They asked me to accompany them to the Regency. Their fingers curled around the polished grain of wood. I didn't bother giving them an answer.

The Regency: walls within a walled city, enclave, oyster-pearl. Sheltered from riot, storm's eye. I knew it, I had even carved it. I had never dreamed of visiting.

Four sets of stone doors opened, each diminishing in scale. I was ushered into what might have been a ballroom and what might have been a bunker.

At the far end of the room there was a crowd. Cheap clothes, the same as mine, linens roughened at the edge. None of us belonged. One man I recognized, dressed in purple, with a forked beard. I recognized him from his self-portrait—the painter Lorgado.

We waited there, complaining first, eventually in silence. The jostling stilled. Our minds ticked over and constructed silent horrors.

For one hour we waited, and then a harried man came out of a hidden door, carrying a stack of papers. These were distributed to us, to all the artists of the city-state. On each was a crude line drawing of an old and rather frail man.

"Florian looks a bit like that," he said, and had us thrown out into the night.

Weeks passed, and the embers of western Phuzein gently cooled. Thin ghouls clambered through the wreck, retrieving broken glasses, a set of marbles, a stump of bone. There were no burials. The city had been cauterized; it came to a dead halt.

Brightly-colored militias padded through bombed-out streets. Florian's rule was much contested.

In Phuzein's living half, the half still breathing, normalcy returned. There was a regent, and a need for coins. The circulation of Auréles could not be prevented, only discouraged. We worked long hours to bring Florian to the masses.

We called Maya my coin-spouse. The workshop was our household, hers and mine. We ran it as equals, her strength and my design. Her body a coiled power, incomplete without the hammer in her grip. She wore it like another fist.

Quintil, who had wasted his twenties on us. He had stayed too long, beloved dogsbody, because he loved us so. He could have taken any job. He had a certain smile, a way of wearing his hair, that terrible thing that people call charisma. It flattered us that he stayed, that he indulged us like a preferred nephew.

He never said how many sugars were in my coffee. Too many, I know that. My life beyond the workshop, in the small brown damp of my apartment, was entirely unsweetened. The hole in my tooth, the sweet ache in my jaw, I owed to him alone.

They sent me to the dentist, in Auréle's final year. He told me I had come too late. He cracked me open wide and pulled out dead enamel and poured in gold to fill its place. Bottom row, fourth from the back.

We called it Quintil's tooth, and it lived inside my head, and I hoped that when I smiled it made me appear charmingly piratical.

Spring came, and we played flick-games once again, and soldiers came to the workshop door. They told us Florian was dead, and I wondered what would be the next to burn.

When the soldiers were gone, Maya asked who I would choose as future regent.

"Lucian," I said, without thinking. Lucian had been Auréle's uncle. I thought I might be able to adapt my old design.

Fig. 3. Bronze coins, 356 P.F. (post-foundation).
Obverse: profile of a woman with curled hair, variously identified, left-facing.
Legend (right): HADRIA REGENT. Legend (left): VITELLIA REGENT.
Reverse: Five-pointed crown.

These bronze phu are in fine and very good condition respectively. Little is known of the short reigns of Hadria and Vitellia. The shared portrait is rudimentary, lacking the detail standardized in earlier coinage. Given the commonalities, Hadria and Vitellia may have been sisters, or even twins. The significance of the five-pointed crown to either sister is sadly lost.

I walked through one of Phuzein's five remaining streets, and dark ribbons curled around my feet. Confetti had been collapsed by a thin rain and coagulated in iron guttering. The remnants of a victory-parade sluiced their way down into the sewers.

Vitellia in triumph, said the writing on the walls. I tried to remember which Vitellia was. Florian's niece, or was that the other one, was that Hadria?

Easy enough, to declare yourself regent. Tyrant of a small and failing neighborhood, nothing else. The truth is there is no Phuzein anymore, or if there is, it is somewhere deep under mud and ash, stamped by the boots of three armies. They have enacted geology, all of them: contributing thin strata of dead, one fossil layer that denotes Auréle, the next Florian, the city of each passing day is laid to rest and compacted into sediment.

All that is left are the parades.

The Regency has been sealed. It sits in a nest of wreckage, a gleaming egg of stone. In the mornings there are men with crowbars, men with curving, specialized tools. The Regency does not admit them. They have not passed the first of its four stone doors.

Perhaps this was Florian's final act. Perhaps there was some special bolt, a secret mechanism that he struck as they dragged him out, as they peeled him away from his sea-shell throne.

Perhaps the men are tired, and do not care to break themselves in opening a bottled tomb.

Vitellia's encampment sits outside the city limits. These days, that isn't very far. Hadria, her rival, has gone underground. Some say her council-chambers float in the echoing drip of the sewers.

I watched the blue-black confetti drain away, and wondered if it fell in wet and heavy clumps on Hadria's desk.

Two self-declared regents: one above, and one below. A city neatly divided by faction. Street cobbles are only a thin barrier, and a porous one. Parades are a holiday from further war.

Somewhere else, Lucian, preaching in quiet words to his Aurélian sect.

Somewhere further still, or maybe dead, or maybe never yet alive, Phuzein's founder, its god-king, who built the city walls and left us to rule as regents in his stead.

One day we came to the workshop and Maya was gone. Her home was long since destroyed. She used to sleep in the workshop, in a hammock that caught the rising heat of furnace coals. The hammock was gone, too, slashed away from the high hooks embedded on the walls.

There is a world beyond Phuzein. I do not blame her for seeking it out.

The coins come from two of us, now. Quintil's shoulders have broadened, Maya's hammer has reshaped him, he has become a foundry-thing. He cropped his curls of hair, the better to withstand the heat. His apartment is gone, and mine as well, we sleep on thin mattresses curled below the hammock's absent weight.

I have never seen Hadria, nor Vitellia. I don't know if anyone has.

For their coins, I drew a woman from my imagination. I used the same for both, I couldn't see the sense in doing two. We used one of my standard reverses, pulled it blindly from a canvas sack. Everybody likes a crown.

No soldiers have come, on any day. There are more urgent things, I expect. All we mint is bronze, lowly single-phu pieces. The city is a ruin. The economy contracts.

"It's very important," Quintil said, his face mock-serious, "that when the soldiers do come, we don't give them the wrong pile of coins." We laughed hacking, smoky laughs at that.

There is no more sugar, or coffee, or takeaway coffee shop.

I scraped the paper ribbons from my fraying boots. I turned past the Regency, past the standard urban dawn of men with tools, prizing at the thickness of its oyster-shell.

There were screams. Louder, metal sounds.

I watched in paralysis as four sets of stone doors opened, one within another. There was smoke, and there was dust, and from it all rode an army, pouring from the opening in stone, an army on horseback, under a blue banner. They trampled over the workers, and they trampled over their tools, and the message on their banner was the name *Lucian* and nothing else.

Fig. 4. Bronze coin, 356 P.F. (post-foundation).
Obverse: unclear male profile, right-facing.
Legend: L () C () A ().
Reverse: plain.

This bronze phu is only partially-minted. Although of poor condition compared to the Lucians of the 360s, it remains a highly collectable piece. The partially printed obverse is indicative of an interruption of the minting process. Metallurgic dating suggests this to be the earliest surviving Lucian on Phuzeian coinage. Lucian is credited with the revival of the city-state following the devastation of the Year of Five Regents. His program of public works earned him the title of "Second Founder."

I spilled over the threshold of the workshop in a clatter of pans.

Quintil was seated on a low stool and stoking the morning's fire. Bronze sheets hung in gleaming racks behind the shaved curve of his head. My mind was going faster than my words, and something caught up in it, reflective. The metal's sheen against the flame, against the perspiration rising on his temples. They triangulated, held me fast.

There was grace within that one momentary eternity. I despoiled it, running towards him, pulling him by the shirt.

"It's Lucian," I said, and the words of it collided with metal and rebounded as a great cry. "He was in the—he has soldiers!"

From the window, the street beyond was empty, becalmed. In every home the same conversation, the same quiet tick of logic and calculation.

Hadria, beneath. Vitellia, on scorched plains. Lucian, in the city's heart. The rusted jaws of old Phuzein had at last closed around us. War would bloom, and we were beyond escape.

Maya was right, then, to leave when she did. Right, too, that I never would have followed.

It would have broken her heart to see Quintil choose.

He was slumped now against a pile of coins, a spill of Hadrias pooling round his thighs, each staring out with a single shining eye. His own eyes were low, unfocused. His muscles seemed to drain away.

"What do we do?" he said to himself, or to the floor.

I sank my way down next to him. It seemed very obvious to me. I thought of Maya, flick-regent of so long ago. She was gone, and Phuzein was lost. What remained was under my design.

"We do what we can," I told him, steeling my voice. "We make money."

Soldiers came, and it might have been a Wednesday, I had no way of being sure. Inside we were all industry. I think that surprised them. I had hunted through my papers, through the stamp-vaults in the underside of my desk, retrieved a primitive draft Auréle. I had seen Lucian, once, years before. Slimmer than his nephew, drawn-in around the mouth. I took my needle-tools and I cut and I shaped and I recreated him, there, in less than one hour.

Quintil struck discs and did his best to conceal the trove of other regents.

When the soldiers came, they were under a blue banner, and I felt pleased that I had made the right decision. "Come in," I said, over the hammer sound. "Lucians, hot off the press!"

Quintil twisted in surprise, his hand slipped—he struck the die and stamp askew, and I winced. Nestled in its mold, a half-coin, misprint, reject. I felt an absurd kind of sympathy.

"We need metal," said a man with epaulettes braided in a powder blue. "For the war."

"Coins," I said, as if in correction. I did not understand that his eyes extended past treasure, onto long sheets of bronze that might tip arrows or form missiles or sharpen javelins to the point of death.

He smiled, appreciative of my remark, and sent a baton cracking into my jaw, dislodging a bloody powder of teeth.

A second crack, harder even, as my head collided with the workshop floor. Somewhere far away an alarm was ringing inside my head. I pushed past it, spat clots, did my best not to choke.

Between the first strike and the second: Quintil in motion, his hand reaching again for the wrapped leather of the hammer's grip.

I would have shouted out, if only I had the voice.

He had it in his hands, he was hefting it as if he had the slightest idea—

The stone slab was ice against the wet heat leaking from my head. I, a smashed thing, watched as a squat soldier calmly disarmed Quintil, pinned him against a far wall.

Just as calm as he swung the hammer into the boy's head.

And again.

Quintil sank to the floor, and the soldier kept the hammer in his hand.

They let me be, after that. They had no quarrel with the gasp and twitch of dying fish. I watched as they stripped my world to the bone. Every coin, every sheet, every disc. They laughed and they joked and then they stepped outside to win a war and bring peace and they even closed the door behind them when they went.

Fig. 5. Gold coin, 356 P.F. (post-foundation).
Obverse: Portrait of a smiling man with cropped hair, right-facing.
Legend: QUINTIL.
Reverse: Beaker with smoke curlews rising (disputed).

This five-sorel piece is in exceptional condition. The design is sophisticated, although its meaning is obscure. The coin is the sole extant evidence for the apocryphal 'Sixth Regent' of Phuzein. His role in the civil wars of 356 remains unknown, as does the significance of the beaker icon depicted on the reverse. Sarazzala (1246, p. 19) suggests "Quintil" as the lost name of the mythical god-king who first founded Phuzein, and reads the coin as depicting an idealized ruler after a year of turmoil and decline. No other monarch is depicted as smiling on Phuzeian coinage.

Someone now dead once boasted that his words would form a monument more lasting than bronze. He had celebrity, of course. Renown. My words will fall in the mud and die like worms, in thin strings. I live a life unrecorded, nameless. I can only speak to the future in metal.

Coins have that power. Do you think the rich need money? What was left that Auréle had to buy? But he is gone, and all those tiny Auréles in the mud are not.

I have built monument enough to the regents of this city. I have preserved their tyrant names. My dying act I dedicate to another more deserving. It saves a name that history would not.

I lie bleeding in an empty workshop, devoid of metal. I expect my lifespan will not extend beyond another day. Riot comes again with fiery teeth.

Devoid of metal, devoid of speech.

Except, amongst the swollen morass of my lower jaw, the red ruptures and the shatter of enamel—

Quintil's tooth shines out in splendid gold.

It has been loosened already. Quick work, to wrench it from its bruised and purple bed.

I assemble my tools: ceramic crucible, lost under a table-leg. An unmarked stamp. My needle-blades, too fine for the craft of war.

Quintil lies stiff and dead against the wall, but that is immaterial. His face is in my mind, there is no need for reference. The way the corners of his mouth tuck up into his cheeks.

I stem the bleeding from my jaw, and tell his story, the only way I can.

ABOUT THE AUTHOR

Louis Inglis Hall is a civil servant living in Scotland. His stories can be found at *Clarkesworld, Strange Horizons,* and *Andromeda Spaceways Magazine,* amongst others. He was introduced to Roman coin tables at university and hasn't been the same since.

Celestial Migrations
CLAIRE JIA-WEN

You say, "Then the celestial manta rays began to come. Astra mobular, mobile through the stars. Most schools didn't even have cosmobiology departments at the time. So we've been operating with limited facilities. Most agree that the megafauna feed in the toxic lake of the 53-Oenone mining colony, but we're more unsure how they found it. The prevalent cultural myth is that migrating bodies can sense each other, the longing for home like an invisible frequency."

The first ray arrives, and Ev and Adri aren't done packing. Faces filthy with grease and mineral dust, the two shove oxygen tanks, Well-Fare-Squares, and balm for Adri's leg into their packs. The lack of light isn't helping. The tiny bunker windows usually don't provide more than a few strands of starlight and an uninspiring sight of Oenone's dust-colored plains; as more giant beasts break synth-atmo, even that little light is blotted out. The shadows stretching across their faces compound their existing exhaustion. Black hair looks ashy, bright eyes dull.

At least the dorm's other eight couples have already vacated. The stale air is only broken by clasps clicking and murmured, "have you taken your stellarmotion sickness pills?" For once, Adri can move through the bunks without scraping an elbow, and Ev doesn't have to roll her eyes at a toddler who's climbed three bunks higher than he belongs. Adri thinks the little buggers are endearing. Ev finds the other parents irresponsible, and frankly, *selfish* for bringing their kids to a fucking mining colony half the solar system away from Earth, away from its schools and purified air; Ev would never lug her child to Oenone like he's some teddy bear she can hug to assuage homesickness.

She'd savor the solitude if it didn't mean they were late. Five minutes before their last shift had ended, one of the mining rigs—metal beasts, really—drilled too deep into the rinocrand bedrock, dislodging a boulder that smashed its fuel tank open. Boss Meng didn't want the thing leaking precious oil through the New Year holiday week, so Ev and Adri stayed to fix it.

"I can stay. You should go," Adri had told Ev. The thought made him nauseous. Not at missing New Year's—Benja would be fine with his mother, he loved Ev—but for the year that would come after. A few years ago, doing a repair similar to this reseaming, Adri had been overcome with the numbing revelation of *I'd rather be anywhere than sticking my arm into a nest of hyperconductors, in a mine that feels like being stuffed inside a corpse.* He wasn't much better than the metal beasts. A wind-up toy. If he didn't get to count the new gaps in Benja's teeth this year, he might topple over and never rise again. *I don't want to do this.* "Your performance review doesn't need this to survive the next layoffs."

"Guma is trying to teach Benja the cultural significance of New Year's dinner. His own father missing it might decapitate the cause before it launches," she replied.

Adri nudged his hip against hers. She passed him a humming driver. "You can admit you don't want to pick the bones from the roast fish by yourself. I won't tell Benja his mom's not great with chopsticks."

You say, "Chūnyùn—the homecoming rush every Lunar New Year when migrants return to usher in the year with their families. We used to be able to call it the largest migration in the known universe. Now, we have to call it the largest human migration in the known universe."

Finally, *finally,* everything has been crammed where it should. Ev and Adri rush out, footsteps ricocheting through the empty dorm. They can't miss the flock's departure. They're not getting off Oenone otherwise. The trans-stellar flight prices might've dropped incrementally after the rays started coming, but the megafauna can't instantaneously correct decades of scalping.

Darkness still blankets the outside. The ground is rarely this free of the rhythm of drilling. The wind is finally audible: whining like it aches for the cacophony of metal beasts. The corpo didn't bother to develop the synth-atmo beyond *livable*, so an acrid taste blooms on their tongues; it stings their nostrils as they run, atmo-suits crunching like foil with each movement. Ev keeps her hand tight around her husband's arm. The atmo-suits' fibercell tech keeps the cold from lancing into their skin, but the flat landscape, punctuated by the occasional tread track, *feels* bloodless. Hollowed out. Oenone is much farther from the sun than Earth.

The sky seems made of the gliding masses, their pale underbellies like a churning layer of clouds. No time to appreciate the megafauna. Ev and Adri trust, pray there are more coming, but they must keep their eyes down. Despite its abundance of rinocrand, or perhaps because of it, the Oenone landscape isn't particularly conducive to human traversal. The brittle ground chips at each of their steps.

And the mine runoff. They studiously avoid splashing into the cocktail of oil refuse, ground-up limbs, and undesirable minerals, even as they trace its path downward, following the indents where other feet, other wheels, trod just earlier.

Adri grits his teeth through the pain: a hot iron pressing deeper, deeper into his hip. His clunky plastic leg has a gift for wedging into invisible cracks. A metal beast crushed his flesh one. He could have a nice neuroprosthetic that responds to mental commands, but it's money that could be put towards Benja's ex-mem upgrade. Adri's leg is gone. Benja's doesn't have to be too. Benja can, *will* be more than a miner.

Benja's mathematical maturity, his teachers say, could be generational. *If cultivated.* When Ev's mom died, Ev used the corpo-issued money meant for the funeral's return ticket to buy Benja a refurbished ex-mem so he could keep up with the kids whose devices could index the universe in a neurochip. Adri likes to joke that the mission is to get Benja engineering the metal beasts that will crush people's legs.

"Is it bad? Do you want to get balm?" Ev asks, though they both know they don't have the time to stop.

"It's bearable. Got all the pain out of my system yesterday," Adri replies, though they both know it always gets far worse before it gets better.

Then Adri's leg snags on a protrusion in the mottling shadows.

You say, "The unknown is understood through metaphor. We have no proof these megafauna are alive in the way we understand alive as a set of conditions to be checked off. Homeostasis. Cellular organization. Energy expenditure. Inheritance of traits. But we have no way to understand these space-faring masses besides comparing them to the living. Scientists, translators, making the alien familiar."

Ev and Adri have always been part of the migration. This is their first time witnessing the phenomenon from the outside looking in. The breath knocked out of Adri when he fell. His oxygen tank flashes green for full, but he still can't get a clean lungful. Their hearts still rabbit from the panic of dislodging Adri's leg from the protrusion, Adri saying *go without me* and Ev only managing to reply *no,* over and over.

The rays take turns swooping, skimming the jeweled surface of the lake swirling with rosettes of oil. Ev thinks that drowning in it would be like an ant floundering in a bathtub of bleach.

Over the years, the migrants have honed the embarking technique to an animal efficiency. The experienced land near the rays' spiracles and clamber into the vestigial pores, sanctuary caverns. Adri prides himself on having the eye for approximating this trajectory, and Ev has admitted, in a moment of relieved delirium, that his frequency of success supersedes random chance.

The unskilled stay where they land. They'd have better luck finding rinocrand ore in zero light than navigating the back of a beast, dappled with infinite blemishes like a holocopy of the stars it came from. So these unskilled, unlucky, latch themselves to the speckled skins like rock climbers, like barnacles. Nothing to do but brace themselves. Pray the atmo-suit keeps adhesion, pray asteroids are kind and avoidant. But barnacles survive the currents of the world too.

It's not often a migrant plummets into the shimmering liquid. It does happen.

It's impossible to dredge up sympathy, or wonder. Not when the last ray descends, and Ev and Adri are not at lakeshore.

This is fine, Ev is already thinking. It's fine. She's mentally drafting a message to Guma. Tell Benja his parents are sorry, but they needed to stay on Oenone, work hard. Just like how Benja should work hard in school.

Last year, Adri held his son in his lap, practicing Benja's information retrieval with battered annotation guides. Was this the last time Benja would be small enough to hold like this? Would he return next New Year's to find an updated version of his son that didn't like or want his dad's company? He reassured himself he had another year. Kids don't grow up that fast.

But it will be another 365 days of Ev's eyes going blurry from diagnostic analyses and Adri dragging his leg across skeletal mineshafts until they see Benja again.

Adri's turning away, and Ev can't stop thinking about when they were seventeen, and she said those fatal words. *I want to keep the baby.* His expression as he comprehended the infinitude of his potential futures narrowing into defined limits. All his dreams would need clauses appended to them: if time allows, if the money is enough to support the family, if you're okay with scheduling it during Lunar New Year, no I'm not free any other time.

"Wait." She grabs his hand. It's trembling. "Look."

A last ray has alighted.

You say, "Maybe the celestial rays are like their oceanic counterparts. Filter feeders. Maybe their stomachs are heavy with stars. For the humans crusting their backs, this is the largest cyclic migration in the known universe; for the megafauna themselves, maybe these annual relocations are only a walk from the nap-pod to the fridge, from fallow space to nutrient-rich nebulae, those schools of infant stars."

A beautiful thing to have held the cosmos inside your stomach, Adri muses. He is not looking at the expanse of streaking stars.

Ev isn't looking at the sidereal blur either. The void is there, the vacuum of all things unknown, and it's boring. With the adhesive function of her atmo-suit plastering her to an endless plane of ray skin, everything bleeds into monotony. A commute is a commute is a commute. Something to be distracted from with audiobooks, podcasts, conversations. Neurochips and ex-mems, for those who can afford it. Before they exhausted their conversation topics, Ev and Adri agreed that their smaller ray likely lags in the flock's wake to ease travel, the others taking the brunt of solar headwind, maybe. They're not scientists; it was a fun hypothetical.

Now, she can't stop thinking about it. The flock moves ahead as one, silhouetted against planets and asteroids and stars and the enormity of everything human minds were never structured to comprehend; easier to think of it as a 2D wallpaper than a thing with infinite depth. Ev wonders if their ray thinks its predecessors have abandoned it. She wonders if their ray will eventually resent the distance, despite the distance sustaining it. She wonders if their ray would rather they all endured the wind together, trading a comfortable life for a communal one.

Ev is good at thinking. She's also good at recognizing when she should stop. "What are you looking forward to?" she says.

"The protesters. Love a chummy welcome party."

Ev rolls her eyes. Rinocrand cultivates a novel bacteria. The novel bacteria trivialize carbon capture, but rinocrand extraction disturbs Oenone's orbital trajectory, and that's reason to harass the miners who see their son once a year. "I'll make sure to convey that to Benja."

Something inside Adri twists. It's the same as when Ev dragged him to the empty classroom after graduation, when he didn't yet know about the life beginning in her belly, the boy and the universe. She's speaking to him but looking slightly away, like she's deliberately untethering him from her consciousness, giving him permission to slip from it and never return. They're hundreds of thousands of miles from shittily painted World War II posters and the smell of cheap beer.

"I understand if you hate me," she'd said.

Adri hates twelve-hour workdays. He hates curling up in a crib of a bunk and wishing to tears that he'll wake up to Mom's weekend French toast and a sky that's blue. He hates Boss Meng. He hates greasing the same metal monstrosity that turned his leg into paste. He hates annual migrations on the backs of beasts who come before he's ready. He hates how his eyes sear when his gaze lines too closely with the sun.

And yet.

Puffed layers of insulation keep him from folding her into him like he did in Mrs. Moore's classroom. So he says, "Evelyn, I understand so little of how this works. Sometimes, I wonder if Benja even exists or you made him up so you'd have company out here, but I come home each year and he's there, and you are too. You've balanced an impossible equation, you know that? Three hundred and fifty-eight days of Oenone for seven days of Benja, and yet the love overwhelms the hell. You make love weigh so much."

Ev doesn't know what to say. Her vision is a soup of blurry stars and the familiar lines of his face, distorted by the glare of a galaxy across his visor. She always felt she should thank him for staying, but it feels weird to thank someone for basic decency. *Thanks for doing the bare minimum. I thought you'd be worse.* But he's made every moment after more bearable. Why not start with that.

Then the ray splits in half, and they are not on the same half.

You say, "Metaphors only take us so far. The reproductive habits of celestial rays diverge from their Earthen analogs. In fact, their similarity to prokaryotic reproduction has led some of my colleagues to extrapolate the existence of gigafauna, though the analogous scale of the latter might eclipse that of our own planet."

Ev spends the rest of the commute thinking. She runs calculations on whether a child can be sent to university on a single income. She can't tell if it makes her a good mother or a fucking terrible wife.

You say, "I'm aware of the recent discussions around rebranding scientists as scientific analysts, because so much of what we do is interpreting what these giant models spit out. But the language processors of our neurochips are only possible through my grandmother's generation, the people who learned English for annotation work. If not for my parents, we could only speculate at the reproduction processes of the celestial rays."

You pause.

You reach for a bottle of water, like the problem with your throat is lack of substance when it's actually the thousand emotions lodged into it.

Your mother won't talk to you anymore.

Your father talks to you once a year: when he tells you he's transferred the New Year good luck money to your account. Every time, there's an awkward pause, like he debates saying the next words. Every time, he says them anyway. "Your mom wants you to know she loves you."

You always say, "I love you both."

You want to explain that if they were distant, never came home for New Year, maybe you would've finished university in four neat years. Got a job at Sesame or Cosmo Corp. You would've engineered translunar liners, or encoded the decision logics of autonomous mineral extractors to optimize worker-rinocrand risk tradeoff. You would've been so good at it.

But they came home. Your mother crushed you to her, more of a dance than a hug because the stellarmotion sickness hadn't worn off yet, so you swayed like drunkards; your father picked all the meat from the fish's cheeks for your plate because the closer to the head, the smarter you'd become, and when you asked why *they* didn't need to be smarter, your mother would tell you she forwent university so she could work with the rays. So *you* could do the learning, she said.

You want to ask why, when the fish was picked to bones and you swirled rice into the residual soy glaze to sate your lingering hunger, they fed you with stories of the rays swimming through space. The humans crusting their backs like barnacles. Didn't they know these New Year feasts sealed your fate—how could you do anything but follow them to the cosmos, rig your sensors and machines to the alien-beasts? It was the only way you could comprehend it, and you need to comprehend it. It wasn't a choice. It wasn't a *choice*.

You've said these words. You still think that if only you say them again, they will understand. You are still a child who buys paper calendars so you can tick off 358 days with a pen you fished from a shuttering antique store.

One eye-click accesses the file, a permanent resident of your ex-mem's recently opened folder: Evelyn saying *why can't it just be a hobby,* and *the other sons bring their families honor and prosperity,* and, voice breaking, *I never wanted you to go to Oenone.*

Those things are why I can't sleep without imagining your dad die.

Murmurs have begun to fill your silence, but the acoustics of this hall are weird, and so is your hearing. Before you were invalidated for your parents' insurance, SmileCorp subsidized three cochlear fluid correction procedures: two for workplace hazards—your parents'—and one you managed to argue was a research necessity.

You've fucked the fluid up plenty of times since then. Maybe that's why the New Year's money has been increasing.

The problem is: they think you should honor their sacrifice, and you don't know how to tell them that this is the only way you can. There is a difference between honoring the intention and the heart of a thing, and they will never forgive you for choosing wrong.

The emotions burn like the cheapest stuff at Erika's—half whiskey, half battery acid, sludging down your throat.

You say, "I'll move into the meat of my thesis now."

ABOUT THE AUTHOR

Claire Jia-Wen is a speculative fiction writer originally from the 626 and has been published in *khōréō* and *Clarkesworld*. A Viable Paradise alum, she is currently a student studying media studies and algorithmic fairness.

Rolling the Dice: Tabletop Adaptations of Speculative Fiction

KYLE TAM

Human imagination can often be limitless, and when it is allowed to roam, we call it fantasizing. This is something we often take pleasure in—an activity that allows us to leave behind the mundane for the extraordinary. Logic dictates that to constrain this imagination would put a damper on our spirits, especially when we are imagining the world that exists to us only on the page. Worlds hidden behind closet doors, manholes, and impossible dreamscapes. And yet, when play is done in a controlled environment, we often find more enjoyment than if our dreams had gone unfettered.

Nicholas Mizer's work in the realm of tabletop RPG development notes that the most notable of games, Dungeons and Dragons, was forged by combining the conflict simulation of wargaming, the flexibility and multiple win conditions of Diplomacy, and the worldbuilding of authors like J.R.R. Tolkien and Robert E. Howard. Furthermore, he finds that this culture of play tampered with rules for long-running campaigns. In this instance, the world becomes the main character instead of the players. This seems especially evident in a world derived from storied bodies of speculative work like Tolkien's, Sanderson's, or Burroughs'—after all, these have already been sites of great adventures and will be so again. It makes sense that they are not only the grand stage for, but a tapestry by which a great history is always being written, one that includes the unsung tales of players at home.

From the medium's nascent beginnings up to this moment in time we see there has always been a desire to inhabit the great worlds of speculative tradition. That is why the natural extension of our desire to inhabit the worlds of our imagination has manifested in tabletop games.

Short of heading off into a closet or being given a revelation of divine birthright, playing a tabletop version of our favorite pieces of fiction is one of the closest ways we as human beings can come to living within the realms of our fantasies and fears.

Likely the most prominent of these adaptations is *Call of Cthulhu*, a work derived from the greater universe surrounding the Ancient Ones. It is divorced from its originator, H. P. Lovecraft, by instead inviting the player in not as hapless bystanders to the great evils of the universe but as Investigators. Titled. Working not only to uncover secrets of the world but to fight back against the cold reach of the stars. But in translating this unfathomable, abstract world and assigning truth, a certain agency has been gained by the player characters. If it can be measured, it can be perceived. And if it can be perceived, it can be killed. The game then becomes divergent from the original intentions of its authors, leaving behind the horrors of the unfathomable and unknowable and entering the realms of a survival horror. Like any adaptation transitioning from one form to another, it has taken on its own traits and its own form, and judging from its unfathomable popularity there is a welcome desire to be able to overcome the darkness.

So, what makes a speculative work adequate for adaptation? If you look at what is available on the market, the one factor that ties all of these licensed works together is that more often than not, they have strong, dedicated, and outspoken audiences behind them. Although there are millions upon millions of worlds that have been dreamed up and printed, there are very few that find themselves converted into a playable form. Licenses are not always easily negotiated, with publishers likely preferring to hedge their bets on speculative works that are known and appreciated quantities. The *Cosmere Roleplaying Game* became the top-earning RPG Kickstarter of all time, in part due to Sanderson's prolific body of work, which has sold millions of copies across over thirty books in the universe—as Laura Hirsbrunner of Brotherwise Games notes, "The Sanderson name is all we need." Other prominent licensed works include *The Conan Role-Playing Game*, *The Lord of the Rings Roleplaying Game*, *The Expanse Roleplaying Game,* and *The Dresden Files RPG*—all household names with eminent staying power and quite notably, other forms of adaptation that have been well received.

But there is also the matter of the depth and breadth of the world. The world of professionally published tabletop RPGs thrives, like any publishing business, on the number of volumes that make their way out the door. Where it meets players is in the player demand for more material to draw upon for the games they play at home. While homebrewed material concocted on the back pages of a notebook is par for the course, one can assume that in drawing from a pre-existing story, the greatest appeal comes from official deeper insight into what makes the world tick. This is especially true when a number of these, including the aforementioned Cosmere RPG, are built on the d20 system. If the system is itself typical when compared to its neighbors, what will distinguish it is the material available for one to sink their teeth into. Locations, non-player characters, playstyles, and playbooks containing previously untold secrets from a beloved universe that unfold before the players, whether in the form of new powers of the Bene-Gesserit or the deeper mysteries of Mars.

Accusations often fly across social media, lurking in idle replies or hidden chat rooms, that using pre-existing systems, such as the native d20 of D&D or another "generic" framework, might make adapted games of speculative fiction or existing IP, uninspired pastiches that slap X theme and Y setting over the same old skeleton. There is an argument that has been made time and time again that it is merely about approachability and familiarity, but a question remains—are these games truly capturing the spirit, the magic, of the worlds that birthed them?

Andy Douthwaite and the rest of the upcoming *Modiphius Discworld RPG* team chose the alternate path, to look towards creating a system that adhered more to the spirit of the Disc than it did to the familiarity of tabletop convention. According to Andy, the game's custom Narrativium system makes use of Traits as applied to dice—in layman's terms, everything that defines a character is relevant when determining what they're good at. All of this while enticing Lady Luck herself and the whims of every variant of polyhedral die.

It's a departure from the original Discworld *GURPS* game, which brought the world of the Disc into the pre-existing *Generic Universal RolePlaying System* of Steve Jackson. *GURPS* positions itself as a roleplaying system in which anyone can play anything in any setting. Through the use of 3d6es and modular characteristics, *GURPS* strips away complexities to create the base framework of any world. While the Modiphius *Discworld* game seems closer to the letter of Pratchett's writings, the spirit of the Disc undeniably lives and breathes in *GURPS* still, carrying comedy in every page.

Of course, this is speaking only of the world of officially licensed games. In the realm of independent tabletop game design, it is not uncommon to find RPGs that seek to emulate and then expand upon the emotions behind speculative works and make them playable. Often these works must have the serial numbers filed off, distinctive enough that they are more akin to mutations of the original rather than derivative. But they are response and admiration of the original works, creating a bridge between the author as a creator to be admired, and as a purveyor of a message.

As The Sun Forever Sets by Riley Daniels is one of these works, drawing upon the original *War of the Worlds* to create an environment where players must grapple with the opening notes of an apocalypse underway. Riley notes that while their original conception of the game was *War of the Worlds: The Game* due to its predominance in the public domain, removing that label from the game meant they had the freedom to stretch the question of how the circumstances of an apocalypse might play out on an individual level. To investigate not only mankind's response to the apocalypse, but also how mankind has been failed by the powers that be, the empires that are in the process of falling- an important question that would be left untrodden in an official game.

Recently, the creators of the Liminal Horror ran the Twisted Classics Jam, which invited creators to draw upon classics from different mediums in order to create new material for this core game. Without the honor and restrictions of an official license, these designers and countless others have begun to build Theseus' ship from the pages of their forebears, both paying tribute to and iterating on what has come before. From a mishmash between Bram Stoker's classic and the eponymous *Hotel Dracula* to a murderous truck that would give Stephen King a run for his money, each creation is a homage, remix, and expansion of the original idea. What makes adaptations like the Twisted Classics, as well as adventures for games such as the Redwall-esque *Mausritter*, differ from a work merely paying homage is that they are reinterpretations, a melting pot of ideas made suitable for play. A benevolent mutation of a "what if" that puts the reader directly into the shoes of what could have been. Through the quantification of foes to face or challenges to be overcome, fantasy becomes a sense of reality. A test with a value can be passed. A foe with a health bar can be defeated.

While this author has their own preferences in whether they prefer tabletop adaptations that adhere to the letters of the world or their spirit, there is still an undeniable disconnect between the world as written and the world as played. A divergence that stems from the need for balances of power, of tabulation and calculation so that players might enter the setting in a way that satisfies the logic of the world. However, there exists a third category of adaptation that breaches the barrier between these two mediums.

A particularly special relationship is created when the fiction of a given world is cemented into the fact of its tabletop adaptations and vice versa. For example, the *Warhammer 40,000* universe is in equal measure a miniatures game, a series of tabletop RPGs, and a universe of books bound together in the Black Library. As the miniatures game progresses forward and backward in time, there are undercurrents of fractured factions and the consequences of momentous events. The powers that be who have designed this world inside and out understand the significance of these records enough to have the in-universe font of all knowledge be given a place in the world. There is a continuous cycle, a feedback loop, although with the vast amount of material on display and the necessity of models to sell, *Warhammer 40,000* is a universe that must move at a snail's crawl lest it one day finds itself with precious little story to tell. Here, then, is the double-edged sword, where the fiction finds itself forced to march not at the pace of a story's natural progression, but by the beat of a corporate drum.

Aaron Voigt is one of that particular group of designers who has written out the mechanics of his world and one of its stories within the pages of *Detente for the Ravenous*. According to Aaron, he chose the medium of tabletop to work in tandem with Detente because it was familiar, but also because he was better equipped to make a unified world that could be adjusted at will. He also notes that in the construction of a story, in the words of fellow tabletop designer Jay Dragon, "the process of game design is simply constructing skeletons for dreams." Tabletop is more forgiving as a vehicle for narrative because it is a collaborative vessel. A novel's narrative can have one narrator, or many, but it is still a singular web of story. But in a tabletop game of dice, tests, and encounters, there is an infinite world of possibility. The game feeds the book, the book feeds the game.

The space that a tabletop RPG adaptation occupies is ultimately the bridge between the world inside of an author's head and that world as reinterpreted by the readers. It is a playground with all the bells and whistles first dreamed about by the author while adhering to its own rules and conventions. Officially licensed games possess the blessing of their creator, emerging fully formed and sprawling with the secrets of their progenitors. Independent games file off serial numbers and interrogate the original premise of a story, not irreverent but inquisitive. And in the blessed middle are the ouroboros', games, and stories which act as reflections and distortions. Endless creation, endless change.

ABOUT THE AUTHOR

Kyle Tam is a dreamer, writer, and full-time complainer from the Philippines. Her games include the IGDN Honorable Mention *MORIAH*, *Primadonna* from PlusOneEXP, and *Forsaken* from Afterthought Committee. She has also written for publications like *Interstellar Flight Press*, *Strange Horizons*, and *Into the Spine*.

Special Arrangements:
A Conversation with Sean Markey
ARLEY SORG

Sean Markey grew up in Charleston, SC until, at age sixteen, his house burned down. "Our family moved to Florida after that, and I left Florida as soon as I possibly could." He went to college to be an elementary school teacher and earned a certificate for teaching in special education. "I initially went the 'becoming a teacher' route because I had illusions of spending all my spare time writing fiction, and I (mistakenly) thought 'oh, I'll just spend the whole summer writing, it'll be The Best!'—Spoiler alert, that's not how that works." He also attended a writing workshop on the Oregon Coast with Kristine Kathryn Rusch and Dean Wesley Smith.

Markey lived in Salt Lake City for several years, then moved with wife Beth Wodzinski to the high desert outside of Moab in southeastern Utah. "It's incredible there, the weathered red rock landscape hundreds of millions of years old. We eventually escaped the drought and the ever-increasing 100+ temps in the summer by moving to this old farmhouse in northern Vermont. It's got a huge barn on the property that used to be a grist mill, and it has its own little pond. It's beautiful and I love it here, even in the winter when it's -20°F sometimes . . . "

In addition to running Psychopomp, Sean Markey earns a living doing marketing-related work. He did spend some time working in education, among other things. "My favorite job was as a person-counter for a newly opened (at the time) commuter rail system running eighty-three miles from Provo to Ogden in Utah. They wanted to get a sense of how popular the trains were, so they hired people to just ride the trains up and down in shifts. I loved that job—I'd have to count people from SLC up to Ogden and down to Provo that got on my car, and then I could just chill on the way back. I'd bring my ancient laptop and work on fiction—as at the time I still tried to write fiction."

Sean Markey took a stab at selling his work beginning in 2005 and landed a couple of notable sales, including "Sorrowbird" in *Fantasy Magazine*'s June 2008 issue and "The Spider In You" in *Strange Horizons* in March 2009. He was also a slush reader for *Clarkesworld* and did some work with *Shimmer*. "At first it was just helping Beth stuff magazines into envelopes and take them to the post office to mail. But eventually it was helping with the website and some of the tech/distribution stuff."

The Deadlands launched in May 2021 with E. Catherine Tobler as editor-in-chief and Markey as publisher. Markey launched Psychopomp in January 2023, with Christopher Barzak's novella *A Voice Calling* as their first book (both print and digital) in March 2024. Stories from *The Deadlands* have received many accolades, including finalists for the WSFA Small Press Award, the Sturgeon Award, and the Locus Award. Tobler received a World Fantasy nomination for her work with *The Deadlands*, adding to her already impressive list of accolades. Psychopomp purchased *Fantasy Magazine* in late 2024 and relaunched the publication as a quarterly under the editorial stewardship of Arley Sorg and Shingai Njeri Kagunda, the former a two-time World Fantasy finalist for co-editing *Fantasy* from 2020-2023, the latter a two-time Hugo finalist for her work as co-editor at *PodCastle*. As a book publisher, Psychopomp is off to a strong start, with work by notable genre figures like Barzak, Vajra Chandrasekera, Premee Mohamed, and others; and having received praise from respected critics in the field.

How did you get into science fiction, fantasy, and similar? Who were the authors or what were the works that you consider to be formative and important to you?

I was way too young for this book at the time, but my mom gave me a Stephen King short story collection—*Skeleton Crew*, and it scared the absolute shit out of me. But I was hooked on it. I proceeded to go and read nearly every single Stephen King book I could get my hands on over the next few years. I constantly got in trouble for it in school, reading when I should have been paying attention or doing classwork.

I got really good at taking tests because I knew if I could finish first, the teacher would let us quietly read until everyone was done. So I'd finish quickly and then spend the next hour or two reading. It was amazing.

It's no surprise to me that the Dark Tower books by King really grabbed my attention. It feels like they mean to me what I've heard other writers say LotR means to them. All of my interest in the multiverse and other worlds and the great, ginormous end of all things comes from reading those books at juuuuust the right age—late high school.

Another writer that's very important to me is Kelly Link. I attended the World Fantasy Convention in Saratoga Springs, NY in 2007. It was my first convention, and I randomly wandered by the Small Beer table in the dealers room. She was there signing books, so I was like, all right, fuck it, I'll pick up a book this lady is signing. I had never heard of her before, I was very new to the non-Barnes-and-Noble side of genre fiction. I picked up a paperback copy of *Magic for Beginners*, which she signed, "love! magic! zombies!" I just now went and looked that up. The book looks like hell. I've taken it everywhere with me, the corners of the pages are all bent, people have spilled wine on it, but I love it. It really blew my mind wide open about what's possible in fiction, and what someone with a strong voice and a ton of creativity can do to and with a story.

It reminds me of a similar path I took with music—I'd been a Metallica fan since like 1992, when I was nine years old, and I almost exclusively listened to Metallica until late high school, when I discovered the band A Perfect Circle, and I was like, *Are you kidding me? You can do this with music?*

So, it was similar reading all this Stephen King popcorn fiction for ten straight years and then reading the title story "Magic for Beginners" in that collection, and it just kind of changed my whole world. So it's a pretty important book for me.

What does it mean to be the publisher for The Deadlands, and is the way you inhabit this role different or similar from other magazines which have a publisher/editor distinction?

I think it's a bit unique. Almost every other magazine I can think of right at this moment, with the exception of *Apex*, runs with the "editor is the publisher is the editor" model. It's obviously a great, smart way to run things. I'd be lying if I said I didn't sometimes wish I was also the editor, to soak up some of those accolades (for whatever *that's* worth).

But honestly that would be an infinite disaster loop. I have big ideas, and I make big things happen. That's great for coming up with cool things to do or try, but really, really bad for making straightforward decisions and being a stable person that meets deadlines. I could never do it. *The Deadlands* would have lasted exactly one and a half issues if I was the only one in charge. I've got a great team that helps me make amazing things happen, and Elise (shout out Elise Tobler!) is extremely responsible for our successes. I also have zero editing skills, and she has ten thousand editing skills, so it's an arrangement that works really well for me—and I hope she'd say the same!

Honestly there are pros and cons to each way. I think the most important thing is that one does a job one is well suited to. I work in marketing and SEO for my day job, so focusing on that for a magazine or a publisher is something I bring to the table. I have put together an amazing team that helps me bring *The Deadlands* and Psychopomp to life (shout out Elise, Nico, David, Laura, Jo, Cory, Amanda, Melissa, Annika, K.C., Christine, Shana, Felicia!).

How did The Deadlands get started, and how did that lead into publishing books as well?

2013 is the earliest I remember being like, *I want to publish books*! I didn't have any money for it, had zero experience, and had no plan. But the interest stayed with me. In 2019 I sold one of the websites I was building for a life changing amount of money, and used some of those funds to continue to build websites.

I did a lot of thinking and journaling for the rest of that month about what I wanted to do with my time. I had worked *very* hard on all these websites. I'm talking sixteen-hour days every day for years, and I remember telling Beth I could just take the next year off—completely off—live on the savings I have, and just explore. What a gift. I'm so lucky to be in this position.

After journaling a bunch, I basically concluded, *Okay! It's time to start a magazine!*

So instead of taking a year off, I got into publishing! And then to make things even more complicated, we made an offer on a house that May (issue 1 of *The Deadlands* was also published that May), and moved across the country from Utah to Vermont with two cats and two dogs in the car with us, at the end of June.

It was an extremely turbulent time to have started a magazine, it turns out, and I just want to say Elise is amazing and the best, because she carried it all through those months.

As to how that led to publishing: much like how authors say, "I want to write books but I guess I have to establish myself as a short story writer" (however wrong that is or isn't), I really want to publish novels, but I thought I'd start with short fiction, since I have had experience working at two magazines, and it seemed a lot more straightforward than trying to publish a book with zero experience . . .

The name *The Deadlands* is from the T.S. Eliot poem "The Hollow Men" ("This is the dead land"). That was Elise's suggestion after a couple weeks of brainstorming names.

The Deadlands has a focus on death, in the sense of "the ends we face here, and the beginnings we find elsewhere." Why this particular focus, and are there challenges that arise specifically because of having this focus?

I've always been kind of fascinated, *definitely* terrified, of the idea of death—from when I was just a kid, staying up late at night trying to process the idea that one day, one actual, real day, I won't be alive anymore. Terrifying. I had never talked to anyone about this at the time, just held it deep inside, and let it grow there in the dark.

I've always been drawn to stories involving death, but also—*most* stories have something of this in them, right? It's one reason I was drawn to Stephen King's *The Dark Tower*. Reading that series introduced me to T.S. Eliot and *The Waste Land*. Reading his work led me to "The Hollow Men", and that really—I don't know. The imagery in that poem stayed with me.

I don't quite know when the idea to do a death-focused magazine came, but when it *was* time to start such a project, the imagery of "The Hollow Men" immediately surfaced and had a big influence over the vibes.

As for challenges that arise, haha, there are some!

At first glance everyone paints us as a horror mag. "Oh, *The Deadlands*? Must be horror." But it super is not! If you've read it, you know this.

Elise and I jokingly refer to it as "*Death Shimmer,*" since these two magazines share an extremely similar aesthetic (and Elise was EiC of *Shimmer Magazine*, so . . . obviously).

We also get a lot of stories submitted where a character dies, but the story isn't *about* death. A death happens, but it's not the point of the story. And that is the biggest difference, the biggest thing people just getting to know us, who haven't read any of our fiction (despite being free online), assume we want to read about in theirs.

Maybe digging a little *too* deep into the marketing side of things, but it *is* harder to publish a specialized magazine. The topic is only interesting to a smaller number of readers. The topic might be too much for some readers, some of the time (when my cat died in early 2022, I thought publishing a magazine about death was real stupid for a couple of months, but ultimately I took comfort from reading these stories and myths about dying and what comes next, and that is also the point of *The Deadlands*). Covers are harder to find, because they have to be so specific. It's all around a harder thing to pull off than just general sci-fi/fantasy (in my limited experience at least).

What are your highlights regarding The Deadlands—what are you most proud of to-date? And what are your hopes and even plans for the future, as far as the magazine goes?

I think, thirty-six issues in at the time of this writing, we have made a very solid reputation for ourselves. We're not well-known in the wider world, but the people that *do* know of us, it seems, respect us.

When I announced that we were opening to novellas (another step on the journey to publishing novels), we received a bunch of really amazing submissions.

I think if I just directly started Psychopomp and said "send me your novellas," we would have gotten some action, sure, but we'd be an unknown quantity, and many writers would not have taken us seriously for the first few years.

But we weren't unknown, we were those people behind *The Deadlands*. We invested in releasing a bunch of really high-quality, big-vibes magazines.

So I guess that's what I'm most proud of to date, the reputation for really great work that we've built.

We also received some recognition, such as having Elise nominated for a World Fantasy award for her editing of *The Deadlands*, or getting a story from one of our first three issues included in *The Best Horror of the*

Year: Volume Fourteen by Ellen Datlow. We've had stories be finalists for the Locus Award and Theodore Sturgeon Award. Every year that they were eligible we had poems as finalists for the Rhysling Award—and one of our poems won (tied) the Dwarf Star Award.

Of course, awards aren't the end-all-be-all goal of publishing, but to get *any* recognition in such a crowded field of ultra talented authors writing unbelievably good stories for so many outstanding magazines—it really makes me happy.

Plan for the future—honestly to keep publishing issues and have our readers like what we do enough to support us. As many people reading this will know, it's tough out there, a lot of good magazines are closing due to not enough support. I know that isn't a super wild goal, but we're still young enough that it's a challenging goal, and what I'm working toward: sustainability, and to keep building a big reputation. You want high quality stories, poems, and nonfiction about death, because that's your jam for some reason? *The Deadlands* is the obvious zine you need to read.

Psychopomp has already published a handful of books in print and digital, including novellas and an anthology. What has been the process for sourcing authors and works so far?

The novellas are all from an open call. In January of 2023 and January of 2024, we opened to novella submissions through the end of April. We will *not* be opening to novella subs in January 2025, because I ended up buying two years' worth of novellas last time we opened. Whoops. There were so many amazing stories though.

The 2024 novelettes were solicited. I reached out to a handful of authors whose work I liked (with input from Elise) and a few of those had the time to write something. The 2025 novelettes—two of which have been announced already, came from a closed call. We were going to publish four novelettes in 2024 and we had three, so I sent an email to everyone we've ever published in *The Deadlands*—fiction, nonfiction, poetry, and said, "hey we need a fourth novelette for 2024, if you've got something send it over!"

We just needed one so we didn't want to open to submissions for 2-3 months or something, and sending to *The Deadlands* authors was a more manageable way to do that, which also had the advantage of sending to a pool of authors whose work we know very literally that we like. That's how we ended up with novelettes from Erin Brown and Natalia Theodoridou. There's one more novelette announcement coming in late spring-ish 2025.

The anthology—*Afterlives: The Year's Best Death Fiction 2023*, which was curated by Vajra Chandrasekera (who wrote the very first story that *The Deadlands* published, "*Peristalsis*") was published in summer last year. I'd had the idea in my head for a while—one thing I love about having a small press that's 100% mine is that I can just have an idea, a wild and outlandish idea like, *what if year's best, but death stories?* and just push it out into the world, brand new.

I met Vajra in person for the first time at Readercon in 2023 and asked him to sign a copy of his *Deadlands* story in our year one anthology. I had been thinking about it, and I thought he'd be the perfect curator for this wild idea I had about a themed year's best anthology, given how often he writes about death in his fiction (and just go to his website and look at the header—vibes are right). He was game, and we made it happen. Year two of this anthology is being curated by Sheree Renée Thomas, who I cold-reached out to and asked if she'd like to be involved, so I'm super excited for *Afterlives 2024* to come out this summer.

You have also published a short story and novelettes on the Psychopomp site. Is this essentially the beginning of a magazine, or is this something else?

I don't think of it as a magazine. Maybe I should? I don't know. I think of it as this weird, undefinable platform of way-cool work: stories, nonfiction, blog posts, music—like a city that grows organically from nothing, and navigating around it doesn't make a lot of sense, vs. something planned in advance on a grid, with thoughtful wide streets, like Paris vs. Salt Lake City.

I like that it can be whatever it becomes . . . music reviews, best-of lists, books or movies or whatever! The downside of this, from a publisher's perspective, is it doesn't get a lot of coverage. For instance, we published a short story by Premee Mohamed on Psychopomp about Voyager I. It's such a fantastic little story that got basically no reviews from any of the regular places that review good short fiction, because it wasn't a part of an organized, ongoing publication. No one was watching for it, anticipating it. So that's one downside we're dealing with currently that I think will fade away as the site grows over time and becomes more known.

The story of how that story came to be is actually an interesting window into what I love about Psychopomp:

I saw a story going around social media about *Voyager I* by Doug Muir, which started like this:

131

"Billions of miles away at the edge of the Solar System, Voyager 1 has gone mad and has begun to die."

And I thought *omg* that is a story I would like to read. Science fantasy is probably my favorite subgenre (see the answer to the next question) and I thought the story of an anthropomorphized Voyager I dying would be a perfect fit for a story on Psychopomp.

I reached out to Premee right away because I knew she would do an amazing job with this, and because we've worked with her previously in *The Deadlands* (and are working on her collection *One Message Remains,* which we are releasing Feb 11th), and because I am genuinely a fan of her writing. I was right, she totally nailed it, and the story really resonated with a lot of people.

So . . . yeah, I don't know what to call Psychopomp—not quite a magazine, more of a living, breathing thing that's undefined.

Do the books published by Psychopomp fit a certain vibe? Do you intend for the line of books to have a certain flavor?

Psychopomp really is a reflection of my own interests. I guess an alternate name for it might be *Markeysworld.* :)

The kind of stories I love to read are the kinds of stories I want to publish. I put together a list for the guidelines when we were soliciting novellas (currently closed!) and it's kind of a grab bag of ideas, like:

- Stories where grief or loss plays a leading role
- Stories that feature the afterlife or the underworld
- Stories that involve the journey through death/the journey of the dead
- Stories that involve death personified (Death!)
- Stories that take place in, or utilize a multiverse
- Stories that involve time travel (esp. those that involve time travel + a previously mentioned theme)
- Space, but make it goth
- A story within a story (within a story [within a story] within a story) within a story . . .
- Stories where things that are not usually personified ARE personified (planets? galaxies? time? . . . bones?)

You can see my preference for science fantasy in that list, but it's not all I want to publish. The stories we publish are on vibes, but this list definitely gives a flavor of the kind of books we publish.

Honestly I'd love to publish more "space, but make it goth" kinds of stories. In early 2024 we published "What Any Dead Thing Wants" by Aimee Ogden, which is about a team of exorcists that visit planets that have been terraformed to banish the lingering ghosts of the native life that's been wiped out, and for me it really carries the banner for what kind of stories I'd like to publish.

What do you have coming up from Psychopomp that you are excited about?

Well, I'm sure readers have just learned about the acquisition and relaunch of *Fantasy Magazine* by Psychopomp, so I'm 10/10 excited for that.

We also recently announced a book/music collaboration with our upcoming novella *Starstruck* by Aimee Ogden, and a similarly titled EP by the band Hail Your Highness. Music is my first love, and since I'm building Psychopomp to be this bizarre and wonderful uncategorizable thing, I'm super excited to start exploring how we can bring music into the mix.

Hail Your Highness is an indie band from Michigan, two sisters creating amazing, dreamy pop. I've been a fan for years now and this past autumn I reached out to see if they would be interested in creating an EP inspired by a *book*. They were game, and Aimee was game, and I can't wait to share the results of this collaboration.

I want to do more of this, specifically with music, but I'm open to other ideas. How can we connect books with other categories of art to make really unique, special arrangements? I don't know, but let's find out!

As mentioned, we have three novelettes coming out this year, three novellas by Aimee Ogden, Josh Rountree, and K.L. Schroeder, then three the year *after* by Bernie Jean Schiebeling, Thomas Ha, and Amal Singh.

In addition to everything I've already mentioned you can also look forward to an audiobook or two, the collected works of *The Deadlands Year Two* and *Three* digital books (we're a bit behind on that), *Afterlives 2024*, the collected novelettes from 2024 (print and digital), the collected novelettes from 2025.

What are your plans for Psychopomp for the next year as well as the next few years?

We're a very small press with very limited funds (and almost everything paid for is paid out of pocket), but I dream big. I'd love to publish a novel around 2027, but we've got some work to do around marketing and distribution (a huge, huge problem for small presses) before we can really take that on.

Also, don't be surprised to see an original anthology announcement in the next year or two. There's an idea I've had in mind for a while that I really want to see out in the world, but that's all I'll say about it for now.

You recently attended a few in-person events. For folks who might see you out and about, whether they are authors or readers, what should they do if they are interested in having a conversation with you?

Approach me. I'm super shy. I will never walk up to people and just start chatting, but I'm always down to meet people and talk about publishing/writing.

Or email me and set up a time to meet. It's easy to remember: sean at psychopomp (you can figure it out from that).

Is there anything else you'd like Clarkesworld readers to know about The Deadlands, Psychopomp and its titles, or you and your work?

If you like what we're up to please support us! Go to Psychopomp. com and buy a book. Go to our Patreon to get an e-copy or print issue. Participate in our yearly October fundraiser where we create a new Ferryman's Coin every year (and have some interesting stuff in store for the next one).

If this is your first time hearing about us, I'd love for you to go to Psychopomp.com, Psychopomp.com/deadlands/, or Psychopomp.com/fantasy/ and check out what we're up to, if you're into that kind of thing!

ABOUT THE AUTHOR

Arley Sorg is an associate agent at kt literary. He is a two-time World Fantasy Award Finalist and a two-time Locus Award Finalist for his work as co-Editor-in-Chief at *Fantasy Magazine*. Arley is also a SFWA Solstice Award Recipient, a Space Cowboy Award Recipient, and a finalist for two Ignyte Awards. Arley is senior editor at *Locus*, associate editor at both *Lightspeed* & *Nightmare*, a columnist for *The Magazine of Fantasy and Science Fiction* and an interviewer for *Clarkesworld*.

Weird and Queer:
A Conversation with dave ring

ARLEY SORG

dave ring was born and raised about twenty minutes north of Boston, Massachusetts. He spent five years at Trinity College in Dublin, Ireland, where he earned a BA in Sociology and Social Policy. He then returned to Massachusetts, spending time in Cambridge and Boston, and earning his MA in Counseling Psychology and Addictions from Cambridge. In 2013 he was a Lambda Literary Fellow. For roughly the last fifteen years he's been living in Washington DC.

A few years before launching Neon Hemlock, ring's first fiction publication was "Eye of the Beholder" in 2015's *Caped: An Anthology of Superhero Tales* (Local Hero Press). He picked up momentum from there, with two pieces published in 2016, four in 2017, and even more thereafter. To-date his work has appeared in places like *Shoreline of Infinity* ("Galaxies of Rotten Stars", issue 17), *Lackington's* ("A Sleepless Hunter's Wanton Fruit", issue 23), *Hexagon* ("Queenmaker Dandelion Stew", issue 10), *Lightspeed* ("The Waking Sleep of a Seething Wound", issue 169), and many others.

dave ring launched Neon Hemlock in 2019 and their first novellas appeared in 2020. He also handles small press logistics with a local nonprofit children's publisher as his day job. "Before entering my double-publishing job era, I worked in a half-dozen nonprofits and government agencies, supporting folks of all sorts. I also chaired the OutWrite LGBTQ Literary Festival here in DC for five years. I feel like I could get into the sordid details of some of the crap I got up to in college, but it might be distracting. Suffice it to say that, in Dublin prior to my visa not being renewed, I was working a day job in a liquor store while pursuing dreams of becoming a fashion photographer and nightclub promoter by night." As both editor and publisher, ring's anthology *Glitter + Ashes: Queer Tales of a World that Wouldn't Die* (Neon Hemlock, 2020) received a Lambda Literary Award nomination, an Ignyte Award nomination, and was a Locus Award finalist; anthology *Unfettered Hexed: Queer Tales of Insatiable Darkness* (Neon Hemlock, 2021) was a Locus Award finalist and won a Shirley Jackson Award.

ring himself received Ignyte nominations two years in a row in the Community category and was a World Fantasy finalist in the Special Award, Non-Professional category for Neon Hemlock. Books by Neon Hemlock have been up for many awards, such as *Off-Time Jive* by A.Z. Louise (Ignyte finalist), *All the Hometowns You Can't Stay Away From* by Izzy Wasserstein (Lambda finalist), *Skin Thief: Stories* by Suzan Palumbo (Aurora and Locus awards finalist), *And What Can We Offer You Tonight* by Premee Mohamed (Locus Award finalist; World Fantasy and Nebula awards winner), and more.

Among his many interests, ring is also into gaming. "I spend a lot of time gaming with fellow writers, which creates another arena to tell stories in. I recently held my first kaffeeklatsch at Can*Con and fully a third of the questions were about collaborative storytelling in TTRPGs. We didn't spend as much time there as we could have, since it was of less interest to the other two thirds of the table, but I love that overlap with fiction, as perhaps is made obvious by the games I keep including in the anthologies I edit."

What were the works and who were the authors that were important to you when you were younger, and why?

I grew up arm in arm with the children's librarians at my local public library and read nearly every book that came in with the blue unicorn "fantasy" sticker put on the spine. I read and reread a few series obsessively: Tamora Pierce's Alana books, Laurence Yep's *Dragon of the Lost Sea* and sequels, Lloyd Alexander's Prydain Chronicles, Ursula K. Le Guin's Earthsea books.

A little bit later, I tore through Anne McCaffery's entire oeuvre, along with Mercedes Lackey, and an absurd amount of Dragonlance tie-in fiction (Team Kitiara). After that, I devoured Storm Constantine, Samuel L. Delany, and Octavia Butler. And at some point in college, I read basically every book described as urban fantasy (in particular Laurel K. Hamilton) right up until—in the romantasy shift of its day— paranormal romance split off from it. I'm ashamed to say I didn't appreciate romance until nearly fifteen years later.

Your personal site shows over fifty original short fiction publications, going back to 2015. How did you get into editing and publishing?

I've always thought of myself as a writer, nearly as long as I can remember. Bruce Coville's *Jeremy Thatcher, Dragon Hatcher* and Diana Wynne Jones' *Charmed Life* are responsible for the thinly veiled fanfiction that was my stapled-and-markered first foray into prose. After an ill-advised period as a poet, I returned to fiction via a 2013 stint at the Lambda Literary Retreat under the mentorship of Malinda Lo and in the penumbra of Samuel Delany and Sarah Schulman. My first published short story, "Eye of the Beholder", came about in the rush of confidence I felt after that fellowship.

Not long afterward, I started volunteering with OutWrite, DC's LGBTQ Literary Festival, and shortly thereafter became the chair of that festival, staying on in that capacity for five years. Publishing came about by accident, as a way towards publishing the winners of a chapbook competition for OutWrite. I had edited my first anthology, *Broken Metropolis*, with Mason Jar Press the previous year. Once I'd created my own press to publish those chapbooks, it made sense to keep editing under that banner. It's all been one long heady rush since then.

What were your goals when you started Neon Hemlock, and what have been some of the major challenges?

When I started Neon Hemlock, I didn't have goals so much as I had enthusiasm, and since then I have amplified my enthusiasm with both anxiety and a fear of losing momentum. Kicking things off in fall 2019 was a strange time to test the waters—my first novellas, *Cradle and Grave* by Anya Ow and *Queens of Noise* by Leigh Harlen, came out in April 2020, which was hardly ideal. Challenges remain financial and logistical—after five years, I've discovered that some of the challenges of running a press have become exponential with growth, even as some become easier from the repetition. I do royalties on a biannual basis and that bookkeeping taxes the limits of my organizational ability, so I'll need to get help there very soon. Enthusiasm has its limits, it turns out.

And then there's the business of trying to make waves within an industry that is geared towards a scale you'll never be able to match. Every other decision is caught between the tensions of acknowledging that impossibility and acting against it.

How would you describe the "flavor" or vibe of a Neon Hemlock title, and what are a few titles you've published which you see as truly embodying that vibe?

I think I answered this question from you in a crowded bar once, so it's cruel for you to ask it again in a more formal setting, but I have quite a difficult time describing this aforementioned vibe! It's hard to know the forest for the trees, I think.

Sometimes I think the answer is *And What Can We Offer You Tonight* by Premee Mohamed, since that's how so many people heard of us. Not too long ago, myself and Premee and some other fine folks were talking to Sarah Gailey about the story behind that book, and it still strikes me as a lovely example of that rare thing of a few souls working together on something singular and then it going out into the world to some fanfare.

Other times I think it's another book—the queer witch anthology I edited (*Unfettered Hexes*) because it took so long to get into the world and had so many moving parts (like the oracle cards illustrated by Matthew Spencer), or *Empire of the Feast* by Bendi Barrett because it was the first novella that I solicited and had written specifically for that solicitation.

How do you usually find authors for Neon Hemlock titles?

The vast majority, especially for novellas, have been through open submissions, though I took a break from it this year so that I could catch up on things. I really love the struck-by-lightning feeling of finding a great story in the slush.

Same with *Baffling*, the flash fiction magazine we put out. 99% of those stories are from biannual open submission. For anthologies, I usually solicit a handful of core authors for the books before I open submissions, partly to signal to other writers the sorts of stories I'm looking for.

What is very recent or coming up from Neon Hemlock that you are really excited about?

We recently finished a crowdfund for *Shatter the Sun*, a sword and sorcery anthology we'll be putting together this year. So that's a new surge of excitement. I also just finished edits on a new novella forthcoming from Lara Elena Donelly that involved a number of unhinged editorial comments—I'm absolutely feral for *Amberlough* and Donelly's subsequent work, so I couldn't be happier to put out this book. We recently announced we'll be publishing L.D. Lewis's novella *The Dead Withheld*, but have only sideways shared that we are actually publishing both *The Dead Withheld* and an as-yet-untitled sequel. So that's quite exciting too!

Neon Hemlock also publishes Baffling magazine, which you edit (and at times co-edited with Craig L. Gidney and Kel Coleman). What is distinctive about Baffling, how would you describe the works you select?

The tagline for *Baffling* is "flash fiction with a queer bent." I'll admit that I don't have a particular idea of what a *Baffling* story *is*. Partly because I always conceived of *Baffling* as being a project that was shared, at one time with co-editors and currently with an editorial team (shout out to Assistant Editor Aun-Juli Riddle and our four rad associate editors). So each issue is more-or-less a product of that shared vision.

With that said, it's usually a little on the Weird side, but can also be overtly genre. The stories' engagement with queerness is sometimes more implicit than overt. Though I often invite authors to make pieces more overtly queer when there's room to do so—it's the sort of place where we are happy to revel in queerness for queerness's sake.

I'm thinking back to early conversations with Craig, my founding co-editor. And one thing we discussed was the idea of having a place where folks knew without a doubt that queerness wasn't the reason their story got rejected. Of course there are a hundred reasons why stories get rejected, between budget and craft and storyline and themes. But perhaps there's something rewarding to know that at *Baffling* it won't be because your story was too gay. Though maybe there's an equal and opposite frustration created—was my story not gay *enough*?—but hopefully the stories we publish with less overt queer themes can address that frustration directly.

For readers unfamiliar with Baffling, if they were to look at two stories, what would you want them to look at, and why?

Let's see. S.M. Hallow's "How to Stay Married to Baga Yaga" was recently featured in Paula Guran's *The Year's Best Fantasy: Volume 3*, so that's a good one! And one of my personal favorites, "To Exhale Sky" by Shingai Njeri Kagunda, is another good pick. The former uses a list to great effect and the latter is a wonderful example of how big a story can be in the small footprint of a flash fiction's wordcount.

You have personally edited a number of anthologies as well. What is your approach to editing, whether co-editing for Baffling, putting together an anthology, or editing books for Neon Hemlock?

I love thinking about things in relationship to each other, both as neighbors in a table of contents but also as the accreted feelings of the stories in an anthology and the resulting pearl—this goes for short story collections too I think, although then I'm not the only one arranging the beautiful objects in relationship to each other, the author is part of that too in a more direct way.

As far as editing itself, I try to be careful about preserving the writer's voice in the face of my edits, especially when I get into the syntactical weeds with them. Ultimately I feel honored to be in a position where I can help uplift someone's words, their craft.

Has editing changed anything about your writing? Does being a writer give you a different perspective than editors who don't also write?

I think it has given me much more practice at endings. Writers will (always?) have more practice at beginnings, especially if you are the sort to jot off a few beginning paragraphs and then get distracted and run off to the next thing. But as an editor, every piece you read and edit and publish has an ending. So you get more comfortable with the shape of a good ending. It doesn't always translate to knowing how to *write* one, but I feel more accomplished at knowing when my endings aren't working.

For folks interested in getting into editing or perhaps even publishing, what is your advice?

Hexagon has a really cool program called Myriad designed to give experience to new editors—at some point I'm going to try and figure out how to do something in a similar vein. Otherwise, I recommend getting involved with a magazine that has an ethos you admire. Read slush—it's such a valuable experience. If you want to do a crowdfund for an anthology, hit me up and I will try to download my various lessons-learned.

I think there's also a need for folks to curate writing in other spaces, like reading series. During the first couple plague years, writer Marianne Kirby and I started a monthly reading series on the Neon Hemlock Instagram that is still going. The writers we've featured have been both stalwarts of the genre and folks doing their first reading. I think the field could stand to have a few more spaces like that—check out *Two Hour Transport* for a lovely example.

You have a collection planned for this year, from Off Limits Press. What can you tell us about the collection?

I'm a morass of indecision and doubt when it comes to my own work—something I try to bear in mind when considering how it might feel on the author side of the fence. I'm really pleased that Off Limits took on this book—it's a selection of my largely contemporary dark fantasy and horror. I would say these stories explore themes of sublimation and dissociation and thwarted yearning. Hewing to one axis of genre felt important when it came to deciding what to include, but it still feels like uncertain alchemy.

The collection includes an original story "Grief Like Rot Beneath the Chassis." What can you tell us about this piece without spoiling it too much?

It's an amalgamation of a grief that I *did* have applied to a relationship that I *don't* have but could have had in my 20s, written amidst the consumption of a lot of gothic fiction. I actually wrote a one-act play based on it where the play ends differently from the story, pursuing the path the protagonist didn't take.

Is there anything else you'd like readers to know about you, your work, Baffling, or Neon Hemlock?

Molly Templeton recently wrote an essay about the difficulties of readers and reviewers learning about the available offerings of small presses, largely prompted by a Neon Hemlock title. I was both gratified by the circumstantial attention that came with the mention and a bit embarrassed that I haven't been able to figure out workarounds to some of the problems she identifies. But I'm so grateful for the readers and reviewers and other community members (not to mention the authors!) who do the joint work of uplifting the stories that Neon Hemlock puts out, because it would be incredibly daunting to do it alone.

ABOUT THE AUTHOR

Arley Sorg is an associate agent at kt literary. He is a two-time World Fantasy Award Finalist and a two-time Locus Award Finalist for his work as co-Editor-in-Chief at *Fantasy Magazine*. Arley is also a SFWA Solstice Award Recipient, a Space Cowboy Award Recipient, and a finalist for two Ignyte Awards. Arley is senior editor at *Locus*, associate editor at both *Lightspeed* & *Nightmare*, a columnist for *The Magazine of Fantasy and Science Fiction* and an interviewer for *Clarkesworld*.

Editor's Desk:
2024 Readers' Poll Finalists
NEIL CLARKE

In late January, we held the first phase of our annual *Clarkesworld Magazine* Readers' Poll for best short story, novelette/novella, and cover art. This is the third year that we have separated short stories from novelettes and novellas. It's more in line with industry awards and it didn't seem fair to pit short stories against the longer works. Since we only publish a few novellas each year (and typically shorter ones), it continues to make sense to group them with the novelettes.

Nominations were collected during a forty-eight hour poll that we announced on a randomly-selected day of the month. The unscheduled narrow window has proven itself to be an effective tool in our efforts to minimize the effects of ballot-stuffing and campaigning. It doesn't eliminate those efforts, but they tend to be easier to spot. There were roughly the same number of such incidents as last year. Overall participation was up by over twenty-eight percent, so even if those votes were allowed to stand, they would have been ineffective at influencing the final ballot.

Judging by the final counts, this was a strong year. Every story and cover received nominations and there was significant clustering within the final standings. There were two-way ties for fifth in both fiction categories and many works missed being a finalist by less than three nominations. In one case there was a four-way tie for sixth, only one point behind fifth.

And the finalists are (alphabetical by title):

"Dandelion" by Marcel Deneuve

"Reminiscence" by Daria Anako

"Robot in a flower field 02" by Ninja Jo

"Secret Garden" by JC Jongwon Park

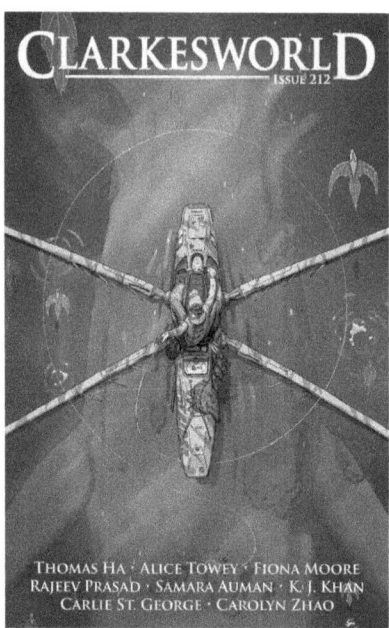

"Strider" by Ilya Nazarov

Best Short Story

- "An Intergalactic Smugglers Guide to Homecoming" by Tia Tashiro

- "Hello! Hello! Hello!" by Fiona Jones

- "Swarm X1048 - Ethological Field Report: Canis Lupus Familiaris, "6"" by F.E. Choe

- "The Coffee Machine" by Celia Corral-Vázquez, translated by Sue Burke

- "The Sort" by Thomas Ha

- "Why Don't We Just Kill the Kid In the Omelas Hole" by Isabel J. Kim

Best Novelette/Novella

- "Fractal Karma" by Arula Ratnakar

- "Lucie Loves Neutrons and the Good Samarium" by Thoraiya Dyer

- "Negative Scholarship on the Fifth State of Being" by A. W. Prihandita

- "Stars Don't Dream" by Chi Hui, translated by John Chu

- "The Brotherhood of Montague St. Video" by Thomas Ha

- "The Indomitable Captain Holli" by Rich Larson

Now it's up to you to pick the winner in each category. Go to:

www.surveymonkey.com/r/clarkesworld2024poll

and rank your choices in order of preference. Voting will close on February 15th at 11PM EST and this year's winners will be announced in my March editorial.

Thank you and happy voting!

ABOUT THE AUTHOR

Neil Clarke is the editor of *Clarkesworld Magazine, Forever Magazine,* and several anthologies, including the Best Science Fiction of the Year series. He is a three-time winner of the Hugo Award for Best Editor Short Form, the 2024 winner of the Locus Award for Best Editor, a four-time winner of the Chesley Award for Best Art Director, and a recipient of the Kate Wilhelm Solstice Award. His next anthology, *Best Science Fiction of the Year: Volume 8,* was published by Night Shade Books in September. He currently lives in NJ with his wife and two sons.

Deploying for a Mission

COVER ART BY HAMISH FRATER

ABOUT THE ARTIST

Hamish Frater is a digital artist living and working in the London area. He started his career as a 3D environment artist at the Sony London studio and is currently Art Director at Hutch Games. He also does freelance work in the TV and Film industry. Hamish's personal work is influenced by his love of old machinery and the idea of human survival in a post apocalyptic world. He prioritizes color, texture, and interesting forms in his work, trying to bring as much life and character to them as possible.

www.ingramcontent.com/pod-product-compliance
Lightning Source LLC
LaVergne TN
LVHW041609070225
802753LV00004B/16